HE KNOWS YOUR NAME
A HOPE SPEAKS NOVEL

DEBBIE GIESE

CROSSBOOKS
PUBLISHING

CrossBooks™
A Division of LifeWay
1663 Liberty Drive
Bloomington, IN 47403
www.crossbooks.com
Phone: 1-866-879-0502

Author photograph courtesy of beckythomasphotography.com

First published by CrossBooks 7/1/2013

ISBN: 978-1-4627-2904-3 (sc)
ISBN: 978-1-4627-2906-7 (hc)
ISBN: 978-1-4627-2905-0 (e)

Library of Congress Control Number: 2013910875

Printed in the United States of America.

This book is printed on acid-free paper.

This book is dedicated to those who need a fresh start.
May you find it in Jesus Christ.

Each of us has a type of unclaimed lottery ticket from our childhood in the pocket closest to our heart. We will need faith and trust to fully retrieve its priceless value. It is not just death that brings pain, but the birth pangs of a renewed hope.

—Francis Anfuso

ACKNOWLEDGEMENTS

This book cover may only feature my name, but I did not arrive at this point on my own. Although a solitary endeavor, writing, at least for me, does not happen without community.

My first thanks goes to the Office of Letters and Light, those fine folks who organize the NaNoWriMo event each year. Without their encouragement to just go ahead and write a bad first draft, I would not be at this point. My characters would still be living in a box in my head. So, thanks guys.

Second, James Scott Bell and his book *The Art of War for Writers* was as much a writing book as it was counseling for those neurotically gripped by fear and self-doubt. I found my own personal pep rally in those pages.

To my friends and family who have encouraged me each step of the way, 'thank you' seems a paltry offering for what you have given me, but it's all I have.

Many friends have offered their time, opinions, and encouragement on this journey. Heartfelt thanks to each of you. Your words gave me courage to keep moving towards publication.

To my family at Fox River Christian Church, you've helped me grow from someone who wasn't sure church was the right place for a woman like me to a woman ready to shout about

Jesus from the rooftops. I can't name you all without leaving someone out, so if you think I'm talking to you, I am. Roots grow deep in a decade, and many of you have held the watering can at one time or another. Thank you.

Shelley Gallamore, you are more than my best friend. You see the good in me when I don't know it's there, and walk with me as I work out the worst, when that's all I can see. You have been my mentor, sounding board, and cheerleader. More than once, you've pushed me to get up and keep going when I was ready to throw it all away.

Julee Oddino, you are confidante and soul sister. You are generous in all things, reading this manuscript with an eye that would make an editor smile. Thank you for believing in me with word and deed.

Jessi, Alex, and Mitchell, my big kids, you lived my hard years where much of this story was born, even if you didn't understand it. I pray that you can see the difference a relationship with Jesus makes in a life when you look at mine.

Connor and Justin, my younger kids, you are the children of possibility and second chances. You see a world of endless opportunity, and help me to see that as well.

To my granddaughter, Sophie, you are proof that time passes in the blink of an eye. You are a beautiful reminder that all of our stories live on.

To my mom, Jan Page, and my sister, Tracy Lemmer, you each have shown me, through your lives, what strong women look like. Your compassion for the world around you inspires me to live boldly for what I believe. Mom, you've supported all of my undertakings. I would not be where I am today without your belief in me. It's contagious.

Rob, you are the love of my life. You are the best husband a girl could hope for, my anchor in a chaotic world. You've sacrificed time, money, and home cooked meals to help me see this project through. I can't wait to see what other adventures await us.

Finally, to my Lord and Savior, Jesus Christ. You are the Giver of Hope, the Rebuilder of all that was broken, the Restorer of all that was lost. You plucked me out of the muck and the mire, cleaned me off, and called me Your own. I pray that every word of this book honors and glorifies You.

CHAPTER 1

Cass Parker puckered her lips and exhaled in a silent whistle, face coloring as her co-worker glanced up in curiosity. *He's never been this late before.*

The phone buzzed in its cradle at precisely 11:14. *Get hold of yourself . . . He's not even fifteen minutes late. Doesn't mean anything.* Cass grabbed the phone before the first ring ended and held it to her ear.

"Sweetie's. 2:30."

"Everything okay? You sound funny."

"I'll just see you there."

At 1:30, Cass's stare burned a hole in Cato Johnson's back as he entered the elevator. She caught the word *dentist* and made a mental note not to use the same excuse when she left. The butterscotch candy wrapper crinkled in her fingers as she struggled to free it, finally just pulling it through the yellow paper with her teeth.

The next forty-five minutes ticked by with agonizing slowness as she rearranged her stapler and counted paper clips, unable to focus on her job as a human resource assistant for Collins & Son, eating two more candies. On a regular day, they quieted her nerves. Not so today. This did not have the makings of a regular day.

Cass shut down her computer and grabbed her jacket. With a smile that did little to conceal her anxiety, she commented to her colleague that she was glad *those* appointments only came once each year.

Caro-*line*, not Caro*lyn*, as she introduced herself, let out a gasp. "What is the date?"

"The twenty-first," she replied, annoyed to be slowed down by small talk. *Get a calendar,* Cass snapped in her head, the tension between the two evident on each of their faces.

"Are you sure? I'm late!" Caroline raced to pack up her desk and made for the parking lot.

Neither of them noticed the concerned looks flying around the room.

Barely able to hear the country music on her radio over the pulse beating in her ears, Cass spied Cato's truck in the parking lot of Sweetie and Harold's, a motel used mostly by truckers coming in off the interstate. *Mostly.*

She pulled in, expertly dodging pot-holes big enough to house her car, no longer noticing the faded plastic flowers in the pots that lined the sidewalks or the missing letters on the Plexiglas sign. Cass was just glad that it wasn't her turn to get the room, remembering back a year ago to the first time she had to secure lodging for their "meeting."

"Driver's license," a woman with impossibly large breasts and robin's egg blue colored hair requested. Her pink blouse had "Sweetie" bedazzled on the top pocket, identifying her as the namesake of the motel. "Overnight or just the afternoon?"

"Overnight, of course," she'd stammered. She couldn't let this woman believe she was the kind of woman who only needed a room for a few hours. Even if she was. "But, uh—what's the difference?"

"Well, dear, if you're out by 5:00, you save fifteen dollars."

"Okay." She swallowed hard. "Out by five", she muttered, turning over her license and her credit card.

"Well, alrighty then," Sweetie chirped. "Enjoy your stay."

Cass knocked twice on the hollow-core door, holding her breath until Cato answered. Once she had gone to the wrong room and had to explain to a man dressed like a giant panda bear that she definitely was not from the agency.

The door swung open and there he was, waiting with flowers. All six feet, five inches of him. Not a small man in height or girth, he often joked "Why would you settle for a six pack when I have the whole case right here?" He ran one hand through his jet-black hair and offered her the flowers with the other. No hug. No smile playing at the corners of his deep brown eyes.

Carnations in hand, Cass entered the dingy motel room, trying as always not to be revolted by the stale smell of cigarettes and the matted-down carpet, the color lodged somewhere between road kill and burnt sienna. Cass's mouth grew dry as he motioned for her to sit. She perched on the edge of the thin mattress, searching his face for a clue of what was to come.

She'd been here before and knew that, by the end of the afternoon, she would either be engaged or alone. In her thirty-five years, she'd seen it go both ways. She'd even made it to the altar once. Cass focused on the picture of a lighthouse screwed into the wall next to the door. Who would steal *that*?

3

Realizing that Cato had begun to speak while a spinsterhood surrounded by cats played in her imagination, she jerked her mind back to the present. "—Can't keep doing this anymore . . ." she heard him saying. He paced the small room as he recited his lines, no doubt having spent the last hour practicing for her arrival. "This isn't about anything you did, it's just that . . ."

Scarcely believing she was getting the "It's not you, it's me" talk, she began to cry. Silent tears at first, hating herself for doing it, then with shaking shoulders and gulping sobs. "When is someone going to love *me*?" she cried. "When do I get to be the winner?" she shouted irrationally, knowing there really were no winners anyway.

Cass heard him apologize for hurting her, although his voice seemed to come from inside a vacuum. His brown eyes held hers captive as he knelt in front of her; she tried to look away but couldn't. She'd never been able to look away from him, even when she should have.

"Hey . . . Cass, right? A few of us are going out after work for a Christmas drink. We'll be at McNabb's over on Erie if you're not doing anything."

As a rule, Cass didn't fraternize with co-workers. In her role in HR, she'd never seen any good come out of it. But, tired of playing by the rules and getting nowhere, Cass pulled into the crowded lot that night and joined the crowd. A brief *"Hey, you came . . ."* was the only interaction with Cato; he had his arm draped around a beautiful woman, her long dark hair hinting at Polynesian descent. Although Cato's eyes continued to follow her, Cass went home that night feeling more confused and alone than ever.

She thought she'd misread him until he approached her in the parking lot, confessing his attraction to her despite his involvement with another woman. Cass took a deep breath and, looking him square in the eye, accepted his offer to "get together" once in a while.

"Cass." His voice intruded on her thoughts. "I didn't mean to hurt you. I shouldn't have let this go on for so long. I . . ." Cato faltered for a moment, the well-rehearsed speech failing him. "I don't want you to hear this from someone else. I asked Mel to marry me."

"You—what? What did you say?"

Large hands reached to envelop hers; shiny dark hair fell across his forehead and she pulled one hand free as if to sweep it back off his brow, but let her hand fall limp. "It's time I quit playing around and settled down. We both knew this wasn't going anywhere anyway." He paused at her sharp intake of air. "I mean, didn't we? Oh, Cass, I'm so sorry."

With no thought to her pride, she dropped to her knees in front of him, wanting to feel his hands in her hair, on her back, telling her he had made a mistake. She waited for the nightmare to end, a contrite apology telling her he was not leaving after all. As she looked at him through swollen eyes, the extra mascara she had so carefully applied in the car leaving black rivers on her cheeks; he bent down to kiss the top of her head goodbye.

Desperate for a chance to change his mind, to remind him of all they had shared over the past year, she lifted her face and met his kiss fiercely, pulling him towards her. Cato allowed himself one last time.

Inhaling her scent, he nuzzled her neck and whispered, "I love you, Mel."

A tidal wave of rage and shame rose up from the pit of Cass's stomach. Her breath came in shallow gasps as she realized that it was over. There would be no calling off the engagement, no relief at the close call they'd had. Cass knew she had lost him.

Slowly she turned to face him. "Cass . . . ."

"Just leave. Just get out. Right. Now. Get out!" Cass's foot stamped the cadence to her orders, not caring that the police would be banging on the door at any moment if she didn't knock it off. She grabbed the pink and red carnations—cheap grocery store flowers—forgotten until now on the nightstand and swung them hard at Cato as he stepped into his tailored trousers, the room exploding in a dizzying array of pink and red carnation heads.

"Cass! Stop it! I'm sorry . . . it was an accident." Cato stuffed his feet into his custom-made loafers and shrugged on his suit coat all in one motion, his shirt and tie all but forgotten. He looked back at her one last time and shook his head as he reached the door. "Crazy—Jeez!" He ducked in time to miss the ashtray whizzing past his head and crashing into the wall as he made his escape. The door shook in its thin frame as it slammed behind him.

Cass looked around the wreckage of the room, wondering what to do next. The pounding on the door relieved her of any further thought and snapped her out of her reverie. Uncomfortably aware of her nudity, Cass grabbed the scratchy coverlet that had fallen to the floor and wrapped it tightly around her full figure, turning off the corner of her brain that remembered those black light revelations on the local news.

She fastened the chain, just an illusion of secur'
and opened the door a crack.

She tried pretending that if it *was* Cato, she
in. Reality spared her of that choice as she was greew.
middle aged guy, scalp peeking between greasy strands of
gray hair combed across the middle. His belly folded over his
belt and hung beneath the sweat stained t-shirt with "Harold"
written in Sharpie on the pocket; his beefy hand clutched a
large ring of master keys.

"What's going on in here? I could hear you's fighting all the
way in the office. Wheel of Fortune is on, for crying out loud.
You gotta go. Right now. And I better not find no damage in
this room or I'll be charging the card. Got it?"

Shoulders hunching to limit his view, she mumbled, "Yes,
you're right. I'm leaving. We, uh, just had a misunderstanding.
I'm sorry." Cass closed the door in his face and turned to face
the room, looking for any real damage beyond the carnation
massacre, before remembering that it was Cato's card that
would be charged.

She retrieved the heavy ashtray from the floor near the
door and stood in front of the television set, letting the weight
of it fill her hand. Cass raised the ashtray and pulled back her
arm, catching sight of herself in the mirror above the dresser.
Wavy auburn hair tangled and standing up like Don King in the
back, ample bosom overflowing the chintz dime store coverlet,
leftover makeup smeared on her face.

Her arm dropped to her side as the ashtray slid to the floor.
The reality of the situation set in.

Who had she become? She didn't recognize that person
staring back at her. Cass pulled on her skirt and sweater,
stuffed her panty hose in her purse, and dragged a hand

7

,rough her hair, a futile attempt to subdue it, leaving Cato's dress shirt and tie where they'd landed a lifetime ago.

A lone light pole in the parking lot tinted everything with an amber glow. Cass walked to her car, the squeal of tires exiting the lot barely registering.

CHAPTER 2

Cass sat heavily in the driver's seat and stared at her keys, wondering which one would start the car. Nothing made sense right now, the temptation to drive into oncoming traffic overwhelming.

She maneuvered the streets on autopilot, the route at once familiar and foreign. Cass halted her car as a stoplight turned red, fumes from the bus in the next lane choking her. A deep breath maybe, she thought. One deep breath and done.

He Knows Your Name.

The partially hidden words of an advertisement on the side of the mud-splashed bus ripped at the pulpy mess that used to be her heart. The words mocked her; nobody knew her name. She swiped at bitter tears that jeopardized her vision, never noticing that the dreary rains of April had given way to the promise of an early spring.

She drove without seeing the soft blue sky streaked with gray as evening settled around her. The streetlights lit up the dusk, pointing out familiar landmarks of convenience stores, big box retailers, and every fast food restaurant imaginable. Cass doubted she would ever be hungry again as the fresh wound of her heartache stirred up nausea in her gut.

Finding herself at another red light—this time next to Chubby's Beer Depot, she followed the flashing neon arrow into the store lot.

Cass caught sight of her reflection in the automatic door, recognizing that she looked like a refugee from an Alice Cooper look-a-like contest. Not caring, she wandered the aisles, unsure what she was even looking for, until she found herself in front of a cardboard display of brandy. *Good enough for the old man, good enough for me.* She set the bottle of liquid comfort and a two liter of 7-Up on the counter in front of the clerk.

"You okay?" he asked, more out of surprise than concern.

Hollow eyes stared back at the clerk, ignoring his overture.

"Keep it," Cass said as she threw a twenty dollar bill on the counter and left, not waiting for change.

Barely braking as she pulled her Dodge Neon into the parking lot of her apartment complex, she chuckled without sound as she noticed a couple jumping out of the way.

Unlocking the door to her apartment, Cass hung her keys on the hook by the door, peeled her feet out of her tan pumps, and made her way in the dark over to the blue and mauve couch no doubt purchased during the height of country chic, brown bag from the package store cradled in her arm. The purring of Stanley, the stray tabby who had frequented her patio step long enough to earn his way into her home, reminded her that she wasn't completely alone. He brushed up against her leg in greeting; she scooped him up and buried her face in his striped coat as a fresh torrent of tears overtook her.

Setting the bottle of brandy and the two liter of soda on the golden oak coffee table—again, a piece leftover from another tenant—she slowly unscrewed the caps off each, realizing too late she'd neglected to bring a glass to the sofa. Too drained to get up and get one, she skipped the soda. Taking the brandy in her hand, she took a long look at the bottle.

Here's to you.

She was unprepared for the burning as the liquor left a trail of fire down her throat and into her belly. "How do people drink this stuff?" she wondered aloud to herself. Stanley perked his ears like he might have an answer, then laid his head back down in her lap. The fire gave way to a warmth that made her cheeks flush, and filled her with a hug from the inside. Encouraged, she took another sip, knowing that the discomfort would give way to heat that just might get her through this night. Alone in the dark, she found solace in the bottle of clear amber liquid.

CHAPTER 3

Cass squinted against the watery light of a new day. Lifting her head, she saw the bottle of brandy on the floor next to the couch, the full bottle of 7-Up on the table, and the memories of the previous day came flooding back.

Now she knew how a jack-o-lantern felt. Guts scraped raw by the liquid companionship from the night before, rivaled only by the intense jack-hammering taking place in her head. She remembered that he had left her.

Not only had he left her, he had called her by the wrong name after making love to her. Of course it couldn't have been making love, because apparently there was no love, but it would take too much effort to sort *that* out. Right now, the only priority was stopping that awful buzzing.

Leaning heavily on the furniture, last night's brandy threatening to make an appearance with every step, she made her way to the bedroom and threw the offending alarm clock against the wall. The noise jarred her head, but the thud and ensuing silence were equally satisfying.

Avoiding the mirror over the bathroom sink, Cass climbed into the shower, setting the dial for as hot as she dared. She scrubbed furiously, determined to wash the shame of the previous day away. Her head didn't feel any better, and she knew with a certainty that she would be sick before the day was over, but at least she felt clean. Wrapping a towel around her body in the chill morning air, she brushed the sweaters from her teeth and risked a glance in the mirror.

Does forgettable have a face? Cass took stock of her reflection. Brown eyes, slightly upturned nose with a spattering of freckles that got worse in the summer, and auburn hair, cut for ease to fall around her shoulders. She skipped the blow dryer and reached for a clip instead. One small step for mankind, she thought sarcastically.

Cass applied her makeup gingerly with shaking hands because even her skin hurt and wondered again how she was going to make it through this day. And the next. How was she going to show up at work day after day and pretend everything was fine, while inside she was drowning? That's the trouble with secrets. The mask can never slip. Ever.

The brandy-inflicted damage repaired to the best of her ability, she hid her puffy eyes behind a pair of laughably big sunglasses and grabbed a butterscotch candy from the bowl on the counter before heading to work, hoping it would settle her stomach.

Turning the key in the ignition, she was greeted by the bell indicating her fuel was low. *Like I need anything else to deal with today.*

Cass pulled into the Quick Mart and filled her tank, trying not to smell the fumes as she leaned against her car. Eyes closed behind her sunglasses, the aroma spoke his greeting before his voice.

"It's on me," the man said, holding a cup of coffee out to her. "You look like you need it more than I do."

Wavering between being deeply offended and insanely grateful, Cass reached for the cup.

"Thanks. Just one of those years," she mumbled, inhaling deeply. She usually had as much cream and sugar as coffee in the cup, but she wasn't usually carrying a hangover the size of Toledo either. One taste of the strong black liquid began lifting the fog from her mind.

"We all have them," he said kindly. "Well, anyway . . ." he stuttered, suddenly at a loss for words.

"Thanks again. I appreciate your kindness." Cass finished filling her tank and opened her car door, relieving him of the need to make small talk. "More than you know," she finished to herself.

Cass pulled into the business park that housed Collins & Son, eyes automatically scanning the lot for the familiar truck, averting her eyes as she remembered what they used to do in it. She parked on the other side of the lot and took a deep breath, steeling her emotions. *I can do this . . . I can do this . . .* she coached herself as she made her way into the glass and steel structure and pressed the elevator button for her floor, mechanically returning the greeting of the security guard on duty as the door closed between them.

The hum of excited voices greeted her as she arrived at her floor. She was unprepared for the small crowd gathered around Cato's desk, looking with admiration at the velvety black box in his large hand. Their eyes locked for a split second. Cato was the first to break the connection.

Choking back the sourness that filled her throat without warning, she turned and raced for the nearest restroom. She could not believe that he would have the gall to do this to her.

Has he always been such a jerk? Was there anything real between us, ever?

Splashing her face with ice cold water did little to calm her nerves, but she couldn't hide in the bathroom all day. Cass pasted on a fake albeit shaky smile, and opened the door, walking smack into Shelby, a woman she had known for a few years but wouldn't call a friend. A pleasant face in the office, perky in that suburban sort of way, but that was all. Cork-screw curls that had to be natural in a golden hue that probably wasn't anymore, sparkly blue eyes, and a dimpled smile. Practically a living Shirley Temple doll.

Cass turned away but not before the other woman got a good look at her face.

"Cass, is everything alright? Not to be rude, but you don't look too good," she said with a sympathetic laugh.

"Fine," Cass replied tersely. "Must be a flu or something." She pushed past Shelby and headed for her desk, anxious for once to lose herself in her work. She could feel Shelby's eyes following her as she made her way across the office. Feigning an air of indifference, she sat down and logged on to her computer, purposely avoiding looking towards the restroom. From the corner of her eye, Cass could still see Shelby looking at her, a bemused expression on her face, and she didn't need to face the scrutiny.

Somehow Cass made it through to lunch, shoulders hunched in a concentrated effort to ward off conversation. Emailing her boss, she told him of her "flu", and took the rest of the day off. Shelby and a few other women in the office noticed her leaving, their eyes meeting once again in silent knowledge. The coincidence of Cato Johnson's engagement and Cass's sudden illness was not lost on them.

CHAPTER 4

Shelby gathered with Caroline and Lauren for lunch as was their custom. The smell of Lean Cuisines and overheated leftovers filled the air as the women bowed their heads briefly over their lunches. Except Caroline.

"Caroline, what's up? You haven't taken your eyes off the elevator since we sat down. At all." Shelby rarely missed anything.

Shrugging, Caroline pasted a smile on her face. "Sorry?" she said as she threw her blue-black hair back over her shoulder. Tastefully dressed as always in one of her trademark silk blazers, she pinned Shelby to her seat with the steel in her dark brown eyes. Tall and lean, Caroline had the air of someone in charge.

"Anyway, did you see how rough Cass looked today?"

"And how happy Cato looked?" Lauren said.

"Cass says she has the flu, but I'm not quite believing her," Shelby said between bites.

"The bottle flu, maybe," said Caroline, flicking her dark hair out of her face and rolling her eyes. "She played with fire and got burned," she said, fiddling with her phone. "Girls like that need to learn."

Lauren and Shelby glanced at one another, surprised by the venom in Caroline's voice.

"You don't play with fire unless you are looking for warmth." Lauren finally spoke up. Her soft Southern lilt masked the steel she was made of. Grabbing her Tupperware container and diet Coke, she shoved her chair back from the table with a vehemence that sent it clattering to the floor. Her low heels clicked her departure.

Shelby ate the rest of her lunch looking at her food. She was too unsettled to risk a glance Caroline's direction. Must be a full moon or something.

No one noticed Cass as she stood at her desk, rifling through some paperwork she'd intended to take home. If she was truthful with herself, she knew she was hoping to run into Cato. He deserved to see just how miserable he had made her. Cass noticed the shade to his office was drawn as she looked down the hall towards his suite. Must be in a private meeting, she thought. Oh well, probably better this way.

She glanced towards the cafeteria and spotted the Ladies Who Lunch, as she privately referred to Caroline, Shelby, and Lauren. What is going on with *them*? Cass was in the habit of eating at her desk, not one to walk up to a group uninvited. She could see that Caroline was riled about something, and Vanilla Pudding Lauren, as Cass called her, stood up so quickly she knocked her chair over.

She had no idea that she was the reason for all the commotion.

CHAPTER 5

Cass turned onto Creekside Drive, the aroma of the chicken rice soup she'd grabbed at the deli filling her car. She'd lived at Creekside Apartments for three years but aside from a drainage ditch had seen no evidence of a creek.

Juggling her purse, soup, and a magazine she'd treated herself to, Cass let herself into the lobby of her building, stopping to check for mail. C. Parker, the raised letters read on the label. No first name, she'd insisted to the manager when she moved in. No sense advertising that a single woman lives alone here. She'd thought about adding Stanley's first initial to the label to throw people off but decided that was just weird. Too much like a crazy cat lady.

"Stanley, mommy's home," she called into the apartment as she always did. The stale scent of spilled liquor assaulted her senses, rushing her back to a place she never visited. Her childhood was defined by two distinct scents: the alcohol her father survived on, and the cloying Sweet Honesty perfume her mother bathed in.

She opened the windows to let in the fresh but chilly April air and carried the offending bottle straight out to the recycling dumpster. Cass hoped the now flat 7-Up still sitting on the coffee table would go nicely with the chicken rice soup.

"*Brrr* Stanley. Stay out of my soup while I grab a blanket." Reaching up high in the bedroom closet for an extra blanket, Cass spotted a faded shoebox on the top shelf. She looked at it for a long moment, then stretched on tiptoe and slid it towards her. She carried the box to the couch along with the crocheted afghan her grandmother had given her when she left home, knocking Stanley off the end table as he slurped her soup.

Cass regarded the shoebox through narrowed eyes, unsure what had possessed her to bring the box to the living room. She packed it up each time she moved only to put it in the same place at each new residence: the top shelf in the bedroom closet. On the right, always on the right.

But she never opened it.

Cass took a sip of flat soda and a swallow of her soup— how many germs can a cat have? It's not like Stanley was a *dog,* drooling all over everything. She regarded the box with the precision of a SWAT team dealing with a ticking bomb. She reached a hand toward the cover, shrinking back before contact was made. Cass didn't need to remove the cover to know what was inside. The contents were written on her soul, proclaimed through her life once again.

She was forgettable.

A mental inventory paraded through her mind: birthday cards from her father through her eleventh year. A collection of photographs, her dad disappearing from them when she was seven. After that, just her and her mom, the pictures reminding her that she looked nothing like her mother who'd been voted the Prettiest Girl in her eighth grade class. The one picture she had from her wedding to Dylan at eighteen. Cass in her lace dress with lace stockings, paying homage to the Madonna era. Dylan in his dad's suit coat and best jeans.

Dylan, who'd talked her out of her virginity, married her when she thought she was pregnant, and left when it turned out she wasn't. Dylan, who couldn't be bothered to put down his cigarette for their wedding picture. Dylan, who showed up in her life long enough to turn her world upside down but didn't stick around long enough to set it right again.

Cass sat on the couch assessing the box and her life, wondering when it was going to start for real.

She hadn't allowed herself to think about Landry Alan Parker, her father, in years. Cass's paternal grandmother, Gramma Eulie, had chosen his name carefully after reading a list of Confederate soldier names. She fancied herself genteel because her name was Eulalie, even though the small southern Ohio town they lived in wasn't exactly the South.

Bakerton, Ohio, boasted of nothing but a steel mill, a few diners, two churches, a stop light, and sixteen taverns. Probably not sixteen, Cass conceded, but more than their fair share. It wasn't the sort of town people settled in on purpose, the Norman Rockwell whitewash concealing the seediness and desperation that permeated the air.

Small towns breed small minds, Cass's mom Geri always said, and Cass was inclined to agree with her.

Divorce had not yet colored the landscape of small town America, and Geri was a threat to the security of every housewife in Bakerton. Cass remembered the whispers in her classroom, no doubt parroting what they'd heard at home. Kids sang "Take out the papers and the trash," pointing at Cass and emphasizing *trash.* Geri was never one to be alone for long.

In the wake of the divorce, Geri and Cassandra, as her mother insisted on calling her, were on their own. It was up to

21

Geraldine Louise Dawson Parker to save the day. She used the only gift she thought she possessed.

Remember, Geri told herself, you were the prettiest girl in the whole eighth grade.

Geri was the originator of the phrase Mr. Good Enough. Cassandra would have a dad for a few months, once even for a year, but they always left. The kind of men Geri attracted were not interested in playing house for very long.

A distant slurping sound brought Cass back to the present as she found Stanley sipping the now cold soup out of her mug. Wow, I must have really zoned out, Cass thought, getting up to carry the cup to the sink. With a heavy sigh, she reached for the radio on her counter. It was meant to be mounted under the cabinet, but Cass hated to drill holes in the cupboards when she didn't know how long she'd be living there. Not that she owned a drill.

"Music for your soul . . . WJSS" came through the speaker as she was searching for a static free station. She went right on past the Holy Roller music, as she referred to it, settling on a country station. Somehow hearing Carrie Underwood sing *Before He Cheats* made her feel better, until she remembered that technically she was the cheatee. *Cheatee. Is that even a word?*

She reached for the dial again, spinning it backwards, and caught off guard by lyrics she didn't recognize, something about a girl two years older and three more steps behind.

Cass reached out with soapy hands and snapped off the radio. She didn't need a song to tell her what a mess her life had become. She could see it every time she looked in the mirror. Every holiday dinner spent at Denny's with her mother.

22

Every time she woke up next to her cat. She was well aware of it, thank you very much.

She drained the water out of the sink, dried and put away her soup mug and glass, turned off the kitchen light, and went to bed with her clothes on, the magazine unread on her coffee table and the box unopened. Cass wondered what the definition of crazy was, not just quirky but certifiable, and pulled the covers over her head. Three more steps behind. The words played over her as she slept without dreaming.

CHAPTER 6

Cass woke well before her alarm, bra straps cutting into her skin and pants twisted sideways around her waist. *Rubenesque*—that's how she saw herself. It had a nicer ring to it than chubby, and sounded classier than voluptuous. *Rubenesque* girls should *not* sleep in their clothes. Peering at the clock through her golden brown eyes, she considered wryly that one shouldn't be surprised to be wide awake at 4:00 am when one goes to bed at 3:00pm. At least her stomach felt better and the construction crew had left her head.

She sat up slowly, savoring the butterscotch candy she liked to start her day with. Something about the amber colored disk soothed her.

Knowing she was not going back to sleep anytime soon, she headed for the shower, grateful that the long slumber had dulled the pain in her heart, even if just slightly. Cass took time to apply her make-up with a perfection that would please Bobbi Brown, styled her wavy auburn hair to bring out its natural curl, and slipped into an outfit that she hoped showed off her curves. If she couldn't have Cato for herself, she thought, he would at least see what he was missing.

All of that effort and it was just 5:30. *Oh well, I can always go in early, get caught up from yesterday, and get out in time to enjoy the daylight.* The days were getting longer and the hint of warmth whispered spring to Cass. For a girl who chose to live in the Midwest, she really disliked being cold. Deciding to splurge on a cappuccino, she stopped in at the Quick Mart. Good thing they are open twenty-four hours.

Same guy working as yesterday, she noticed. Without choosing too, her eyes automatically scanned his left hand for a ring. Bare. He commented that she didn't look as rough as she did the day before, and she left with a spring in her step. At least someone notices me, she thought.

Cass tapped on the glass to get the attention of Roberto, the night watchmen. Roberto was a student at the local community college and worked third shift to pay his rent and tuition. He made Cass feel a little like Mrs. Robinson in the *Graduate.* She was anxious to get busy, looking forward to burying herself in her work for a while. No one better apply for a public relations position today, though, she thought grimly. Those resume's might find themselves in the bottom of the cyber pile. Cato can find his own staff.

Taking his own sweet time, Roberto sauntered over to unlock the door, giving her an appraising glance. Cass pretended not to notice, ignoring him as he complained about no one sleeping anymore. She didn't know what he was talking about until she got off the elevator at her floor and passed Caroline's office. Through the blinds, she could see her at her desk, hands clenched tightly in her hair.

April 23rd. Caroline knew the date was coming but thought she would be ready this year. She woke before her alarm went off, fingers tightly woven through her hair. "I'm going to wind

26

up bald if I don't stop this," she chided herself. Ever since she could remember, she'd pulled her hair in her sleep.

Haunting memories of that day greeted her, requiring no special invitation. The day her husband dropped the bombshell: he was leaving her.

"For whom?" Caroline hissed, drumming her talons on the marble countertop. She was not going to make this easy.

"That's not important. You don't know her anyway. Carol . . . Caroline. Here's the thing . . . I'm tired of living like this." He exhaled deeply.

"What's that supposed to mean? Like what?"

"You know what I'm talking about." Taking a deep breath, Steve continued. "You never let me in. You're cold. A man needs . . . companionship." He chose his words carefully, knowing this was an issue for her.

"You son of a—how dare you!"

"She's pregnant."

Caroline had run at him that day, perfectly manicured nails raking his face.

She knew this was God's revenge on her. She just *knew* it. Steve grabbed her by the wrists, her hands held easily in his, and led her to the sofa. He brought her one of her tranquilizers and a glass of water, kissed her on the head, and left.

The rest of their relationship had been handled through attorneys. Caroline took some time off work to regroup and never went back. She had enough money to live comfortably, and her therapist said she would kill herself if she didn't slow down anyway. Caroline wasn't sure that wasn't a viable alternative.

She couldn't believe four years had passed since that day; her carefully constructed facade of control crumbled once each year. She had done everything right. How dare that girl steal everything she had worked for. She took small satisfaction knowing they both had to leave the firm after their indiscretions were made public.

What was *she* doing here? Caroline questioned as she saw Cass pass outside her window. Thoughtfully she toyed with her phone which was always within arm's reach. At least that would be resolved shortly.

Cass noticed that the shade was still drawn to Cato's office. *Must have left in a hurry.* She unlocked her bottom desk drawer and removed her laptop, grabbing her second butterscotch candy of the day. I could probably drop a few pounds, she thought to herself, if I skipped the candy. Oh well. That would be her only vice going forward. She was done. Done dating men who were not 100 percent available. Who needs this? *Especially considering I brought it on myself.*

Cass was grateful for the early start and clear head she had since sleeping for what felt like nineteen hours. She was caffeinated, rested, primped, and curled. Everything needed for a productive day, at least in her mind. She was checking the background of the third applicant of the day when she felt rather than saw a shadow fall across her desk.

She looked up and found herself staring into the face of Barney Fife. Well, not really Barney Fife, but that was the name she used for the Executive Vice President of Employee Relations, Silas Rollinger. She didn't need to crane her head back too far as his bug bulgy eyes were just a few inches above hers, despite the fact that she was seated at her desk. Typical short man syndrome . . . rocked back on his heels trying to add lift. He probably had a chronic stiff neck from keeping his chin raised that extra inch, like anyone was fooled. He was five feet five inches in his dress shoes, and 130 pounds soaking wet. Still, he was at the top of her totem pole and she needed to show him some respect.

"Sir?"

"Ms. Parker, would you have a moment?"

Not waiting for an answer, he turned on his little heel and headed down the hall to a conference room in the honeycomb office space. He waited for her to sit, the door closing behind them with a click.

"Ms. Parker, let's cut to the chase. I've become aware in the last twenty-four hours of an indiscretion taking place. And while this is not a terminable offense for you, I am disappointed at your lack of judgment, especially considering your role in human resources."

Cass was grateful for the chair supporting her because otherwise she was certain her knees would be knocking together. She did her best to meet his stare evenly, not giving away anything. Not that she needed to speak. The slow flush working its way up from her collar bone to her face was speaking loudly enough to both of them.

"Sir, I'm afraid I need more details. To what are you referring? Has my job performance displeased you in some way?"

"Ms. Parker, I am well aware of the er . . . , the situation between you and Mr. Johnson. You know this company frowns on inter-office romances. It detracts from the professionalism we expect from you, and distracts from the job we hired you to do. As I said, this is not a terminable offense for *you*. But this will result in documentation in your private record. I will expect you to use better judgment going forward. As for Mr. Johnson, as a member of the Director's Board, this is a terminable offense. Mr. Johnson is no longer employed with this company, effective as of noon yesterday."

The air grew thinner as Cass struggled for composure, all the poker strategies going right out the window. Fired? Cato? How did anyone find out? They had been so careful. On one hand, it would make it much easier not to have to think about him now that he was out of the office. On the other hand, she was ashamed to have been caught in this position, even if it wasn't entirely against her employment rules. *I'm sure I'll be drafting a policy change,* the irony of the situation not lost on her.

Mr. Rollinger got to his feet, signaling the completion of their meeting. It would not have surprised Cass to see him shape his fingers into a V and point from his eyes to hers, in a universal *I'll be watching you* sign. He led the way out of the catacombs and went straight to the elevator without another glance in her direction. Anyone watching would not have confused this purpose of this meeting for a promotion interview; this was clearly a disciplinary meeting.

Cass proceeded directly to her desk, cheeks flushed with shame as she considered her options. Quit and look for a new job. Stay and wait until they find a reason to fire her. Stay and do the best she could, resolving to never do anything like this again. *Seriously girl, where's your dignity? No one else knows. Don't give Rollinger the satisfaction of quitting. Revenge is a dish best served cold, and it wasn't Rollinger she wanted revenge on anyway. Stay still. Stand strong. See what happens. I still can't believe Cato is gone. How did they find out? Must have been darn good proof if he didn't fight them on it.*

Caroline watched from her office, eyes narrowed in anticipation. Watching Cass gather her belongings was going to feel like vindication, today of all days, the anniversary of the day she lost to her competition. She played with fire, got burned, and would lose her job as a bonus. Caroline couldn't have asked for anything more. She waited, eyes trained on Cass, until it became clear she wasn't going anywhere.

"Silas. Caroline. Why is she still here?" she snapped into the phone. "Wasn't there enough proof?"

"I can't fire her for that. I'm sorry Caroline. You are going to have to get your cheap thrill another way. Cato is gone though, and I wish I had never seen those pictures. It won't be easy to fill that position with someone of his caliber."

Caroline slammed down her phone, drawing the attention of those closest to her office.

Cass had the distinct feeling all that slamming had something to do with her.

CHAPTER 7

Spring warmed into the promise of an early summer. Cass couldn't help but feel her spirits climb along with the temperature. Work had settled into a predictable rhythm. The brief uproar caused by Cato's sudden departure died down. With no new gas, the fire went out.

"Cass, would you like to grab some coffee?"

Cass looked up in surprise to see Vanilla Pudding Lauren. Lauren, she corrected herself.

"Um, why? I mean, sure. But, why?" she stammered, unaccustomed to being asked to do anything.

"No reason. It's a gorgeous day and it seems a shame to spend it sitting in the cafeteria."

"Agreed," Cass said with a smile. She logged off her computer and stood to stretch.

"I can't believe it's almost summer. We are almost past the point of the latest recorded snow storm. After that I'll put my boots away."

They shared an easy laugh as they rode the elevator to the lower level and walked out the front door. Cass bumped right into Caroline as she exited the building. The other woman made no comment and kept walking into the office complex.

"I don't think she likes me very much," Cass said.

"She doesn't warm up easily. She's really all bark, once you get to know her."

Lauren didn't elaborate, and Cass didn't feel comfortable prying. The questions hung heavy in the air.

"I can't help but wonder why, after two years, you are asking me to coffee. Not that I mind . . ." she stammered awkwardly.

"Cass, I'll be honest. You remind me of me. And you really weren't available for coffee until recently." A quick glance revealed no malice in her expression.

Cass sensed the woman's kindness and reached for it; she was tired of bobbing in her ocean of solitude, trying to prove she was strong enough to handle anything that came her way. On a gut level, she knew Lauren was someone of integrity, someone she could confide in.

"Yeah, it's been hard. You know, sometimes we just settle for what's easy and available when we get tired of waiting for what's right. Not that I wasn't hoping for more. I knew what I was getting into. Doesn't make it right. I know that."

"Hey Cass, I'm not judging. We all do things that in a perfect world we wouldn't do. This isn't a perfect world, however. Never will be."

They walked the two blocks to *Caffeinated,* the coffee bar on wheels that parked near their office; Lauren treated Cass to a Sunrise Cappuccino, with a little sun made out of froth on top. Sure beat the overheated cafeteria coffee, even if I had to have a little therapy session to get it, Cass thought as she sipped her treat. *He needs to check his expiration dates,* Cass thought, as her stomach rebelled against the contents.

Cass began to look forward to their occasional strolls over lunch, finding the woman an easy listener and wise companion as well. There was just something different about her new friend, something she couldn't quite put her finger on.

Driving home with the windows open, Cass sang along to the radio. She hadn't felt that light-hearted in months. If she was honest with herself, not since before Cato. She was always waiting for something while in their relationship, never settled enough to just enjoy it.

Cass never saw the car that broadsided her as she drove across the intersection. T-boned and most likely totaled the officer would tell her later on, at the hospital.

"Lucky she had a seatbelt on . . ."

"How many weeks?"

"Ms. Parker . . . can you hear me?"

The voices floated in and out of the fog that encased her. Like a swimmer trying to break the surface, Cass struggled to break free of the effects of the accident.

"It smells like when grandma died," she said to no one in particular.

"Ms. Parker, can you hear me? You're in the hospital. You've been in an accident." The nurse tried to draw Cass out of her disorientation. "Do you remember anything of the accident yesterday?"

"Yesterday?" Cass yelled."Yesterday? I don't—wait, I was driving home. I was singing. I don't usually sing." Cass knew she wasn't making sense, but it was all she had.

"Ms. Parker, you've sustained a concussion, but as far as we can tell so far, you are very lucky. Your baby is doing fine, and you don't have any broken bones. You'll be sore, and you'll need to take it easy for a bit, but you are a very lucky woman."

"Wait. Slow down. You must have my chart confused with someone else's. I am not pregnant. And the way my neck feels, it better be broken, so you can fix it for me." She tried to say this with a laugh, but it came out more like a sob.

"Ms. Parker, Cass . . ." the nurse began. "Do you not know you are pregnant? We draw blood as a matter of protocol when someone unconscious is brought in alone, and a pregnancy test is routinely part of the assessment for female patients. She turned her chart towards Cass, as if to prove her point.

Pregnant.

Cass never knew it was possible to feel hot and cold at the same time, but there it was. Her face burning, needing to pull the blanket tighter, not sure if she should laugh or cry. She read the notes again.

Cassandra L. Parker, the chart said.

The box next to the word "pregnant" checked.

Oh. My. Gosh.

Rapidly blinking back tears, Cass heard her ask about a Mr. Parker. "We searched your cell phone but didn't find any ICE number." At Cass's blank stare, she clarified, "In case of emergency. ICE. We've been waiting for you to rouse so we could contact someone for you."

"No. No Mr. Parker. There's . . . no one." No way were they calling Geri right now. Maybe there was one person, but Cass wasn't sure. Was their friendship actually a friendship? So far she and Lauren had been friendly but not friends. Does that make sense to anyone but me, Cass wondered. How do I explain to this woman waiting for an answer that I am completely alone in the world? At least as alone as I have orchestrated things to be. Well, not completely alone, she thought wryly. I have a baby inside.

Cato.

Oh my gosh, Cato. What is the protocol for this sort of thing? Since his firing, no one had heard anything from him. Their last meeting hadn't exactly been one of planning for the future. He was pretty clear about that.

Alone, except for Cato's baby. Her baby. *Her* baby. After all this time, a baby. The dream was alive, even though she couldn't feel anything. A dream reborn is a dream that never really died. A resurrection of sorts, she supposed.

Cass snapped out of her reverie, one she deserved, she thought, to see the nurse looking at her, lips pressed together in a line.

"I see. Well, we prefer not to release you on your own at this point, although we can't force you to stay. Are you sure there's no one we can call?"

"Cass, call anytime" Lauren's offer echoed in her head. The smell of antiseptic was beginning to get to her, and she really wanted to go home to her own apartment. She wondered if cats worried and what Stanley was thinking.

"Hand me my phone, please." Cass determined to start a new life in honor of the new life within her.

The new life within her. Hope swelled, crushed quickly by panic. New. Life. A baby. Babies need things. I cannot wrap my head around this, Cass thought unsteadily.

Cass dialed the number to the office while the nurse gathered some pamphlets for her. Pamphlets for pregnant women.

Because she was pregnant. She started to shake again.

"Lauren Downs, please."

After a few bars of the Beach Boys, Lauren answered. "Hello. Lauren Downs." She said pleasantly.

"Lauren, it's Cass." Relief surged through her, taking her by surprise. She began to weep into the phone, horrified that she was doing so but unable to stop herself.

"Cass! Where are you? I've been wondering what's happened. No one has heard from you."

"I was in an accident. Yesterday, apparently . . . no, I'm fine. My neck is sore and I have a goose egg on my head, a slight concussion, but I'm okay. Mostly. Hey, I didn't know who else to call. My car is totaled. I hate to impose, but is there any chance you can pick me up after work and drive me home."

"Of course. Thank you for calling me. Do you mind if I bring my husband? My car is in for an oil change and he is picking me up later. He can grab us both."

"OK," said Cass, oddly disappointed. As the news of the baby was sinking in, she was looking forward to telling Lauren. Now, with the husband coming along, it would have to wait. "I will see you later then. Thanks."

Cass spent the rest of the afternoon watching game shows and how-to's on TV, marveling at the life she carried inside her. She pictured a tiny pink kidney bean, safely sleeping in a little aquatic nest. Cass knew there would be questions and stares, and she would have to tell her mother at some point, but for now, she was enjoying this quiet little miracle. Her little miracle.

Growing up, Cass knew of her mother's issues with miscarriages. It was no secret in their house that she was supposed to have three brothers. It felt a little macabre to talk about, so the knowledge blanketed the room like the plastic slipcovers.

The nurse arranged for the hospital's obstetrician to check in with her. Dr. Jacobsen, as her badge read, told Cass to

HE KNOWS YOUR NAME

make sure to rest, get plenty of fluids, and not to lift anything heavier than a gallon of milk for the next week or so. "Things look stable, but if you start bleeding or cramping, call us. There won't be much we can do at this point except make sure you are healthy going forward."

"Thank you, doctor."

"Ms. Parker," Dr Jacobsen began, "Your business is your business. I understand there was no Mr. Parker for us to call. I don't know what your plans are, but do you understand your options?"

"Options?"

"Options related to unplanned pregnancies. Adoption. Abortion. Here is a brochure if you would like to receive confidential pregnancy counseling. To discuss your options."

Black spots clouded her vision as the reality of what the doctor was saying became apparent. Rage and indignity filled her.

"Dr. Jacobsen, this pregnancy might not have been planned, but I do not need *options*." She said evenly. "I don't know where you get off deciding what *options* I need to discuss"

"No offense intended, Ms. Parker. I just needed to be sure you had all the information necessary. Follow up with your regular doctor in a few days. Good luck with everything."

Still fuming over the good doctor's insinuations, Cass didn't see Lauren waiting in the hallway as the doctor left the room.

"Hey . . . everything OK?"

Cass sat up slowly and swung her feet to the side of the bed, holding the rail for support. She winced as she turned her head to meet Lauren's smile, grateful for the older woman's appearance. She was ready to get out of there.

"Stiff and sore. My bottom hurts from laying on it. And," she paused, not even sure how to say the words out loud, "Apparently, I'm pregnant."

Lauren couldn't keep her eye brows from flying up to her hairline. "OH!" she said in surprise. "I mean, congratulations?"

Cass laughed for the first time in days. "Yes, congratulations would be good. This is a surprise, but it is good. It is good." She knew she sounded like she was trying to convince herself, but she was excited. She had waited a long time for this. Her whole life, it felt like.

Cass and Lauren rode the elevator down to the main driveway, Cass in a wheelchair despite her objections. "You need to take care of yourself," Lauren said. The unspoken *especially now* hung in the air.

"We are right here," she said, pointing to a silver gray sedan. "Mike, this is Cass." Lauren made the introductions as Mike came around the vehicle to take the wheelchair back to the entrance.

"Cass, we can drop him off at home and I can drop you off second to help you get settled, if you would like."

Exhaustion taking over, Cass was grateful for the overture. Somehow knowing that she wasn't going home completely alone was comforting. Windows open to the late afternoon warmth, they made the drive in silence, Cass even dozing off for a moment. She couldn't remember the last time someone had driven her anyplace. It felt good to just relax.

"Cass. Cass . . ." Lauren's voice broke her out of her short nap as she asked for Cass's address. "Oh, you're not too far from our church. I know where that is."

Saying goodbye to Mike, Lauren joked that Cass could stay in the backseat and let herself be chauffeured. "Don't get used to it. Your chauffeur days are right around the corner," she laughed kindly.

Cass handed Lauren her keys and warned her of Stanley, the attack cat, as the woman opened the door to her apartment.

Cass surveyed her apartment through Lauren's eyes, wondering what she would think of it. She'd never had friends over, and her mother was always after her to finishing moving in, in her words. "When are you going to put pictures up, Cassandra? It looks like a lobby."

Cass's apartment was clean to the point of being sterile. Her mother was right; it *was* like walking into to a reception area from a 1980's movie. None of her personality, just the appearance of life. She instinctively knew that more would be changing in the next nine months besides her waistline. She couldn't bring a baby home to a lobby.

"What a lovely apartment, Cass!" Lauren gushed, southern charm covering her shock. "Have you been here long?"

"No it's not, and yes, I have. About three years. It does look a little empty, doesn't it?"

With a noncommittal shrug and a grin, Lauren asked Cass if she kept any tea in the house. "How about I fix us a cup and you go change into something more comfortable than yesterday's work clothes?"

Cass went to her bedroom, calling for Stanley on the way. The tabby poked his head from around the corner, obviously annoyed at his near abandonment. "Stanley, come here to mommy," Cass called, amazed anew at the fact that she would be a mommy to more than her cat. Feeling suddenly younger than her years, Cass couldn't help but be excited. A baby on the way, existing without her even knowing about it.

Not an it, she corrected herself. A little boy or a little girl, she didn't care which. Knowing the trouble her mother had carrying boys, though, she hoped it was a little girl. A daughter she would raise to be confident and strong; she knew she would have to get there first in order to show the way.

"The water's boiling, Cass. Do you mind if I just rummage to find what I need?"

Unaccustomed to having someone take care of her, Cass felt oddly comforted by the interaction. "Go ahead. Cups are on the left. Tea is in the pantry, in the wire basket that hangs on the door." Cass grabbed Stanley to sit with her, and headed for the couch, wondering how to make small talk.

"So, what does your husband do? Mike, right?"

"He works at the church we passed. He's a pastor." Lauren waited for the silence, and was not disappointed. She had gotten over the discomfort her husband's occupation sometimes created, especially among those who didn't attend church. It would have been easier to say he was a counselor, businessman, teacher, public speaker, or any other part of his job, but figured it was best to be up front about things. She'd also learned over the years that she had a built in conversation starter to matters of faith.

"Oh." Cass said dumbly, not sure where to continue. She hoped she hadn't said anything stupid on the way home, trying to remember if she'd cussed or anything. She and God weren't exactly on speaking terms, not for a long time.

"Hey, Cass, don't be weirded out. He's a regular guy who happens to love Jesus and work for a church."

"Was it that obvious?" Cass laughed, accepting the cup of tea.

Lauren nodded before bringing up the elephant in the room. "So, Cass, this baby. Does this have anything to do with Cato Johnson?"

Cass's blush confirmed her suspicion. They had not progressed to the point in their friendship, but Cass knew that Lauren was aware of more than she let on. Sitting together with Shelby, Caroline, and Lauren at lunch was filled with the banter of the newly acquainted. Surface chatter, hometowns, favorite recipes and the like.

"This baby has everything to do with Cato Johnson, and nothing to do with Cato Johnson." She said determinedly. "He made it clear that I am not his choice. He's marrying Mel, and truth be told, I don't really want him back. I think I was a little blind in all that."

"What about your family? When are you going to call them?"

"It's just me and my mom; my dad left when I was little. No one has heard from him in about twenty-five years. I wouldn't know where to find him, or if he's even alive, for that matter. My mom, now that is a story for another day. I'll call her. Just not today."

Not wanting to endanger the growing bond, Lauren didn't ask any more questions. Her years as a lay counselor at their church had taught her a few things, and knowing when to back off was one of them.

"Are you hungry, Cass? Would you like me to send out for anything?"

"No. It's funny, I haven't felt like eating lately, but I usually don't eat as much in the summer. I just figured it was related to that. Not in a million years would I have thought I was pregnant." Not wanting the afternoon to end, she opened up a bit. "My mother had trouble staying pregnant, and when I was not able to get pregnant, I assumed it was related to her trouble."

"Did your mother ever look into that?"

"No. My parents weren't the kind of people to go looking for answers. Not to say we were simple people, but we were simple people," she joked. "I grew up in an industrial town, the kind where the men worked and the women stayed home with the babies. Very little has changed from generation to generation. Typical small town living. My mom married my dad to get out of her house, and I married Dylan to get out of my house. I was pregnant, got married, found out I wasn't, he left—to make a long story short," Cass finished with a shrug. "I guess I'm not that different from them in that regard."

"I'm from a small town too," Lauren said by way of connecting. "It's funny. People think of Norman Rockwell postcards, but it's more like Monet. Things shift depending on the light. Or Picasso."

Lauren looked like she wanted to say more, but left it at that.

"Hey Cass, I'm not going to say anything about the baby to anyone. Not because I think you have anything to be ashamed of, but because this is your news. Share it when you are ready." She stood, taking her tea cup to the counter.

She came back to hug Cass, telling her not to get up. "I'll let myself out. I know you have phone calls to make—to insurance people, not bugging you about your mom," she laughed. "Call me when you are ready to come back to work and I will pick you up if you don't have the car situation sorted out. Actually,

do you want me and Mike to look for a car with you? I hate
dealing with salesman on my own. It's the only time I pull out
the girl card."

"How about this weekend?"

"Mike works all weekend, but one night this week works if
you're up to it."

"Oh, yeah. Sorry. The church, of course. Sure. How about
Thursday night?"

"Sounds good. I'll let Mike know to put on his no-nonsense
face. Let me know if you need anything from the store in the
next few days. I'll be in touch. And Cass . . . I'm glad you called
me."

Cass sat on her couch, snuggled in a light blanket, not
because she was chilly but because there was security in
the action. She mulled over the events of the past twenty-
four hours, most particularly the events of the past six hours.
She had gone from a woman with a car to a woman with no
car and a baby on the way. With a friend even. Not one to
look too closely at things because they had a tendency to
evaporate, she considered that the accident might actually be
a good thing. Not a good thing that her car was totaled, but
she wouldn't have found out about the baby and she wouldn't
have reached out to Lauren.

She did find it curious that Lauren didn't try to get her to
come to her church. Most times, meeting someone who is
religious like that, they want to convert you, to get you to be
more like them. Cass knew it was because she wouldn't fit in.
She'd been there before, growing up in Small Town USA. The
people who went to church were the people with money. The
people with regular families. People like her and Geri didn't fit

in. They'd tried it a few times, at Christmas and Easter, trying on the guise of normalcy, but they didn't have the right clothes or social standing to make it.

Cass could feel the whispers and the eyes on them. "Isn't that Geri? I heard Lan left her." The tongues wagged as the women held their men a little tighter. Cass also didn't miss the looks the men gave her mom over their wives' heads. There was an invitation in those looks; Cass didn't want to consider how many of those invitations her mother accepted.

She did remember the school bus from that Baptist church in the city. Each summer, it parked near the school and housed a little Bible School. VBS, they called it. Pictures of Jesus to color, and if you went three times in a row you got a Bible. The teachers asked Cass if her mom knew where she was and Cass had said yes, despite the fact that her mom was at work and Cass was under orders not to call her unless there was an emergency. From the age of nine, Cass was pretty self-sufficient. She knew how to fix chicken soup for herself if she was home sick, and could find her way to three different parks in the summer months. She knew which neighbors would invite her in to watch TV and which neighbor would invite her in with no thought of TV on his mind.

Anyway, Cass was grateful that Lauren hadn't pulled the church card; it saved her the trouble of having to explain that she wasn't the kind of girl people welcomed to their pews. Made her sad though, because that Jesus had gentle eyes in the pictures, although His dad was a tough character, as she remembered from the few sermons she'd heard. Not the kind of guy you want to cross, and Cass knew, she had crossed him plenty in her life.

Safe in her cocoon wrap, baby safe in his or her cocoon, Cass dozed peacefully, changing position every now and again to give her neck some relief. Tomorrow she would have phone calls to make, doctors to find, decisions about how to explain this at the office, whether or not to call Cato. She realized she didn't even know how to get hold of him; his cell had belonged to the company. Lots of things to think about, but for tonight, she was content to rest.

Butterscotch candy dish within reach . . . what could be better than this, she thought to herself with a smile. Cass hadn't felt this settled in her apartment, her home, ever. In her mind's eye she could see picture frames filled with images of a chubby smiling baby dotting the walls and tabletops. "The journey that lies ahead . . ." she thought as she dozed.

Lauren considered this odd turn of events as she drove home that evening. She prayed as she drove, seeking God for wisdom. "Lord, give me the right words to say to Cass. Help me lead her to You. Bring peace to her mind and comfort to her body as she deals with this news. A baby, God! A baby! Lord, I pray that you will use this little one mightily in her life. In Jesus Name, Amen."

Lauren couldn't wait to get home and share this news with her husband. Mike was a gentle man, and something told her that Cass could use an example of a decent guy in her life. Even if he happened to be a pastor.

CHAPTER 8

Cass did not have to imagine what it felt like to be at sea as the nausea settled in. This is going to be interesting, she thought, as frequent trips to the restroom began arousing curious glances. Not the least of which were from Caroline, whose office door she passed on each trip.

Cass could tell who was heating up what leftovers in the microwave. It almost like a party game—Name That Overwhelmingly Nasty Smell in Three Whiffs or Less. The smell of certain laundry detergent, and sadly enough, coffee, were enough to send Cass's stomach roiling. She wondered how long before her coworkers guessed her news.

Not that she owed anyone any explanations. It wasn't exactly like she had a social circle.

Backing out of the bathroom stall, paper towel held to her lips, she ran into Shelby. Literally, smack into her.

"Oh, Cass, I am so sorry," the Shirley Temple doll laughed. "We need to quit meeting like this."

"Um, yes, excuse me," Cass mumbled, hoping the recent bout of nausea was not evident.

"And again, you are not looking too hot. Not still fighting that flu, are you?"

"No, I mean . . . maybe. I don't know. I'm just not feeling too well." Cass stammered, looking for a way out of the conversation. She splashed some water on her face. "I'm sure it's nothing to worry about."

With that, Cass left the restroom and went down to get some fresh air.

As the mother of two young children, Shelby considered herself somewhat of a pregnancy whisperer. She would tell her husband while watching television, "You watch. In another few months, that woman is going to announce her pregnancy. You just remember that I told you first. Hmm . . . mmm . . . that woman is pregnant. I can tell by her face. It looks fuller. And her chest. Stop looking. Just trust me on this," she would tell him. And 99 percent of the time, he would have to admit she was right. Yup, that girl had a gift. She just *knew*.

And she just knew that Cass did not have the flu, food poisoning, or the Bubonic Plague. That girl was pregnant. Shelby looked over at Cass's desk, and seeing it empty, went to meet Lauren and Caroline for lunch, scarcely able to keep the grin off her face.

"I started a spin class last week at my club. Guaranteed to keep my butt at the top of my legs where it belongs," Caroline was saying as Shelby approached.

"Guess who's pregnant?" she blurted out before either of them could even say hello.

Lauren looked up sharply. "What?"

"Guess who's pregnant?"

"Shelby, did the person who is pregnant tell you she was pregnant?" Lauren had been counseling Shelby on her tendency to gossip, knowing firsthand the destruction that such a habit could wreak.

"Well, no," Shelby answered sheepishly. "But I can't help it if I just have a feeling about these things." She knew she was wrong to continue the conversation but needed one last shot. "Can I at least get credit for knowing ahead of time? I do have a knack for this."

Caroline's eyes narrowed as she searched for Cass's auburn hair across the office. No way, she thought to herself. No way.

"On second thought, I think I will grab a quick walk. Such a beautiful day out." Caroline stalked out of the lunchroom.

"Just breathe. Just breathe." Caroline tried some of the anger management techniques her therapist had given her. "Imagine myself on a deserted island, my—Oh!"

So focused on her breathing and wishing to be anywhere but where she was, Caroline walked headlong into Cass.

"You will not get away with this!" she snapped before she could stop herself.

"Excuse me?"

"Nothing. Nothing." Caroline muttered under her breath.

Cass made her way back to the building wondering what exactly she had done to push Caroline's buttons this time. Seemed like no matter what she did, that woman just did not like her. *At least I don't feel like puking.*

Cass fished in her purse for the referral her regular physician had given her for an obstetrician. She called for her first appointment, initially taken aback that they didn't want to see her until she was officially twelve weeks pregnant.

"What about making sure everything is going well?"

"As long as you are still pregnant at twelve weeks, things are going well. I apologize if that sounds flippant, but if something were to go wrong at this point, there isn't much anyone can do. I'll send you out a brochure with what to expect over these next few weeks until you come in, along with the insurance paperwork. Please call us if you experience anything abnormal. We'll see you in mid-July."

Cass hung up the phone, wondering what could possibly be normal about her situation in the first place. Called by the wrong name, dumped, pregnant. Seriously . . . she'd be happy for a little bit of normal to kick in.

Patting her abdomen, she spoke softly into the air. "Looks like it's just you and me, little one."

CHAPTER 9

The next four weeks flew by in a whirl of seasickness, panic attacks, and excitement. Since her car accident, Cass felt like she'd been dropped onto an alien landscape or twilight zone. Between learning about the baby, the blossoming friendship with Lauren and Shelby, and missing the companionship of Cato, whatever that had been worth, she hardly recognized her life anymore.

"Ms. Parker, the doctor will see you now." A petite Hispanic girl with a quick smile and dark eyes motioned for Cass to follow. "I'm Lilliana. You will see me at each of your visits. I work directly for Dr. Basara. Let's get your height and weight over here," she said, gesturing Cass to a triage station. "Next, here is a specimen cup. We will need a urine sample each time you come in. We are checking for excess protein and sugars in your urine, just making sure you are metabolizing everything in a way that is healthy for your child."

She handed Cass the cup, directing her to follow the chart on the wall for a clean catch. Cass followed the directions, exiting the restroom with the cup wrapped in a paper towel.

"You can just leave it in there each time; let's head down the hall to the exam room."

Cass was instructed to disrobe and put on the fashionable, Lilli said with a smirk, dressing gown, opened to the front. "The doctor will be in shortly."

She sat on the edge of the exam table, eyes perusing the literature lining the walls. Diagrams of what was taking place in her body, nutrition and exercise charts, breast exam posters. Her line of sight zeroed in on the baby's developmental chart. Cass was amazed at what had taken place in her baby's development already. Before she even knew he was there, he had a beating heart, a brain, and the beginnings of a spinal cord.

Hearing the tap on the door brought her attention to the present. "Cass? I'm Dr. Basara. It's a pleasure to meet you." Tastefully dressed in slacks and a sweater, Dr. Basara gave an air of confidence and competence. Cass found it difficult to pin down an age, but guessed her to be in her forties or early fifties. Thick dark hair pulled into a French braid with strands of silver woven through out, she was striking in her beauty. Wire frame glasses gave her a slightly studious look, but the ready smile dispelled any feelings of aloofness.

"So, Cass, tell me about yourself. Have you any other children?" She scanned the questionnaire Cass had filled out while asking questions, drawing Cass out. It helped with the exam if her patients were not tense, and an unplanned pregnancy definitely had potential for tension.

"No, this is my first."

"Does your family have any history of complications in pregnancy?"

Cass told her about her mother's problems carrying boys to term. "I was the only successful pregnancy my mother had."

"We will do some screening and see what we find out when we do our blood tests for this visit. Now, Cass, this first visit involves a pelvic exam, but for your subsequent appointments, we will only measure your abdomen and listen to the heartbeat. As long as you are measuring correctly, you are gaining the appropriate amount of weight, and the heartbeat sounds strong, we will be satisfied. At eighteen weeks we will schedule an ultrasound to get visual confirmation that your baby is developing properly. Lie back please," the doctor directed, helping Cass to support her back in the process. The physician had a lyrical way of speaking; Cass expected to see melody notes dancing around her head like a cartoon character each time she spoke.

Dr. Basara had long tapered fingers, warm on her skin; her destiny was either to be a musician or a physician, Cass thought to herself. She proceeded to palpitate Cass's uterus from the outside, feeling for size and placement. Satisfied, she took a small tape measure from her pocket and measured from the top of Cass's pubic bone to the fundus, or top of the uterus, explaining that at each appointment they would chart the increase. The obstetrician removed an instrument that Cass recognized as a stethoscope except that it had a cone shaped attachment on the end.

"This will help me hear the fetal heart tones. A normal stethoscope does not have the power to pick it up, but this funnel on the end amplifies the sound. In a moment you will get to hear it as well." With that, the doctor danced the stethoscope around Cass's abdomen until she found the placement she was seeking. She listened, brow furrowed in concentration. Uneasiness began to build in Cass's heart until at last the doctor smiled and said, "Your turn."

She took a small apparatus with a speaker on one end and a wand on the other, almost like a walkie-talkie. Cass flinched as the conducting gel oozed its chill onto her belly. A faint whirring filled the air as the doctor placed the wand on Cass's belly. She waited to hear the drum beat of her baby's heart until the doctor told her that the whirring *was* the baby's heart beat.

"Any earlier than twelve weeks and we have trouble isolating the fetal heart tone from the other noises produced in your body. By twelve weeks, though, the rapid swishing sound, as some compare to a washing machine, is evident as a separate sound. A miracle in the making."

Tears squeaked out the corner of Cass's eyes; a part of her, yet separate and distinct. Her baby playing the music of its life inside her own. As constant as the waves of the sea she thought, as she imagined her unborn child tethered safely inside her own body. "It's beautiful," she said, wiping her eyes. "I never thought I would experience this."

Dr. Basara completed the rest of her exam with as little discomfort for Cass as possible. "You may see a few drops of blood after your exam. This is nothing to be alarmed about. Your cervix and uterus are rich with blood flow to sustain your baby's life."

The doctor gave Cass some literature on diet and exercise, cautioning her to limit her calories to healthy ones. This is not the time to go crazy, she said with a smile. She instructed Cass to listen to her body, to rest when needed, and to stay hydrated in the summer heat. "From my exam and the date of your last period, it looks like we will meet this little person on or around January 23rd." Dr. Basara looked up from her chart and met Cass's eyes directly. "Cass, I see from your paperwork that you are not married. Is there a partner sharing this journey with you?"

Shaking her head rapidly, Cass confirmed the doctor's question. "No. We broke up before I knew about the baby." With a rueful smile, she elaborated slightly. "This pregnancy came out of our last meeting together, when he told me he was marrying someone else. I don't know what the legal requirement is, but I don't feel that telling him would serve anyone's best interest, at least right now." Cass looked down at her ring-bare hands and cleared her throat. "He made it clear that we were through. I don't want him to think I would use a baby to try to get him back, and to tell you the truth, I don't really feel like sharing this with him anyway. I feel like this is a gift for me." She didn't say consolation prize exactly, but the thought crossed her mind.

She imagined herself on a crazy game show with a host saying, "For your parting gift, Cassandra, you may choose a pair of diamond earrings or a baby." She would have chosen the baby anyway.

"I understand, but you may want to check out your options legally. You are entitled to financial support of your child from the father, but that would most likely open up custody questions. At some point you will need to address this." She handed her a pamphlet to add to the stack she already had, outlining her legal entitlements and responsibilities. Cass shoved the papers in the side of her purse, glad she had twenty eight more weeks to sort some of that out.

Well, Cass, you survived your first prenatal check up, she congratulated herself. Probably need to call your mother one of these days. Cass dressed, setting up her next appointment for the following month on the way to the lab.

57

Looking out the window in the hallway, Cass watched all the cars heading different directions, and took in the people jogging in the park and waiting at the bus stop. Everywhere she glanced she was struck by the sheer amount of humanity that filled her gaze. Each person with a story to tell, lives to be lived, each separate from the others but inexplicably intertwined. A big cosmic crazy quilt, that's what it is. She felt an affection for her fellow travelers, known and unknown.

Smiling with genuine warmth, she announced herself to the phlebotomist. Apparently the woman with the syringe was not having a fuzzy day as she jabbed around Cass's arm looking for a vein to relieve of some blood. Taping a cotton ball in place, she muttered that the doctor would be in touch. No news is good news.

CHAPTER 10

Caroline caught her reflection in the glass door to her office, and resisted the urge to put her fist through it. Staring at the blinking cursor and rubbing her arms, she fumed over the unfairness of it all. At five on the dot, she clicked out of her computer program and stepped into the July sunshine, oblivious to the warmth on her face.

Always well dressed, she carefully removed her jacket and hung it up on the travel hanger in the back seat. Smoothing her blouse and skirt, she slid into her Mustang and listened to the engine purr. Caroline had heard once that the true definition of meek was strength under control. Barely under control was more like it, she thought. Anyone glancing in the window would have spied a well dressed business woman, cool despite the heat, calm despite the rush hour traffic. Those who knew better would have said calculating.

On the edge again, possibly.

"Pregnant. Doesn't that just figure?" Rationally, she had to admit that Cass probably didn't plan for this to happen, but rational was not a word to describe Caroline of late.

Caroline blinked in surprise as she saw that her car sat in the parking lot of the all-night pharmacy chain that dotted practically every corner in her town. She knew why she was there, even if it had been a long time since she'd made this purchase.

Her feet carried her to the cash register of their own accord, supplies chosen without conscious thought. Driving home with one hand protectively cupping her purchase, she hummed a tune she knew as a child, something her dad used to sing to her, after.

Pulling into the darkness of her underground garage, Caroline grabbed the bag and locked the car behind her. The rest can wait, she thought to herself. Or someone can steal it. Whatever.

The stainless steel fixtures in her kitchen gleamed as she poured herself a Scotch. Neat. She sat on a stool at the breakfast counter, tracing circles in the marble pattern she had requested when furnishing her condo. Everything in her condo complemented the glacial palate she favored, a reflection of the ice that gripped her soul since childhood. Sterile. Clean. Cold. No surprises again.

Surprises are destructive, meant to give power to the one holding the strings, and Caroline was sick to death of someone else holding the strings. Like a marionette with a sharp pair of scissors, she was ready to cut herself free.

Caroline reached for the paper bag from the pharmacy, retrieving the contents one item at a time. The bag of cotton balls. The bottle of alcohol. The band-aids and antibiotic ointment. The stainless steel razor blades. She lined everything up on the counter with the precision of a surgical nurse readying the OR for the attending physician, except that she would be the one making the cuts today.

Torn between the knowledge that she had made a promise to never do this again and the intense desire to regain some sort of control over her life, Caroline surveyed the scene in front of her.

Her hands shook as she unbuttoned her blouse and hung it carefully on the stool next to her, taking a seat in front of her arrangement. Caroline closed her eyes for a long second, knowing there was still time to turn back. She didn't have to do this.

She picked up the razor, its metallic scent filling her nostrils. No one knows what beauty lies in simplicity, Caroline thought to herself. The singularity of its design meant to fulfill one purpose: to cut cleanly.

Before she could change her mind, she swabbed her arm with a cotton ball doused with rubbing alcohol.

Caroline lifted the blade to her bicep, watching the trickle of blood fill the path the razor traced. A short gasp gave away the sting, but with it came the release she'd been seeking. By the time she'd left four fresh stripes, she didn't even notice the sting, mesmerized by the blood running down her arm onto the towel in her lap.

Shame, sadness, defiance . . . all mingled with the blood as it flowed from her wounds. She hadn't done this in so long her therapist stopped asking. Caroline knew that cutting wasn't the answer. But somehow, once she was on the edge of it, turning back was impossible. The flirtation always ended in death. As soon as the thought found its way to her conscious mind, she knew she was incapable of resisting. Like a drug, she thought. I am no different from the addicts.

Aware on some level that she was destroying her body as some sort of revenge, she didn't have the courage yet to think it through. The scars she kept hidden repulsed some, and the pain she caused herself was pain she wished she could have caused others.

Cutting was a poor substitute for justice.

The release that accompanied the cut was short-lived, the emptiness she sought to fill waiting.

Caroline carefully folded all of the supplies, the unused razors, the sterile dressings, and the ointments into the expensive towel and carried the package to the linen closet. Taking the sheets from the shelf, she slid the bundle onto the shelf and replaced the sheets in front.

She smiled at herself in the mirror as she passed, lips stretched tight over her teeth, looking more like an animal, leg caught in a trap, baring its teeth in warning to anyone foolish enough to come close.

So be it, she thought, as she went to dress. So be it.

CHAPTER 11

Cass sat on her couch, phone held in her hands. Just tell her, she coached herself. You are a grown woman for crying out loud. What is she going to say? She looked at the phone one last time, giving it a chance to ring and buy her a little more time, then dialed her mom's number before she changed her mind again. Cass knew it wasn't fair to her mother to put this conversation off any longer.

"Hello?"

Cass sucked in her breath, ready to blurt out her news.

"Hello? Who's there?" Her mother's voice sounded old and thin, alarmed by the silence on the other end. *When did that happen?*

"Mom, it's Cass . . . Cassandra," she said, in an effort to start the conversation on solid ground. "No, no, everything's fine. Hey, do you have a minute?"

Hearing her mother's answer, Cass began. "Mom, I'm not sure how to tell you this, and at my age I probably shouldn't be so nervous . . ." Her mother's excited chatter interrupted her.

"No, mom, I'm not getting married. But I am having a baby. It's a long story."

Cass shared the events of the past few months with her mother, surprised at the compassion in her voice. She wasn't sure what she had expected, but it wasn't understanding. With relief came hope. Maybe she and her mom could begin fresh with the birth of her mother's only grandchild.

"I've decided not to tell him. Not sure if that's right or wrong or even legal, but he made it clear that I am not his choice and I don't see any reason to involve him at this point. I can take care of both of us just fine. He didn't want me before, and I don't want him to think I'm looking for a hand-out. Besides, I wouldn't even know how to find him."

She answered her mother's questions, assuring her that she was under good prenatal care. "Mom, I told the doctor about your miscarriages. She ordered some tests and couldn't find anything that would indicate a problem."

"Well, do we at last know if I'm knitting pink or blue?"

"Go yellow, mom. It's too soon to tell anyway, but I figured I might as well keep the surprises coming," Cass said with a laugh. "Take care, mom. Maybe you can come for a visit in the fall when it cools off. You can sleep with Stanley. Don't worry, he's my cat," she explained at the alarmed response.

Despite the growing friendship between Cass and Lauren, Cass still found herself spending lunches on her own. The warm days beckoned her outside, and she was grateful that the architects who designed the grounds took into the account that open space is good for the soul. Walking the paths, watching the life surge around her, built a connection to the life surging within her.

Even though she was just thirteen weeks pregnant, she could feel a difference in her abdomen. It felt like a promise.

Full, sacred, not quite there yet, but not just an illusion. Holding her hand down low, beneath her belly button, she could feel a compact hardening of her uterus and knew that something brilliant and amazing was going on in her body. Besides the fact that her already full-breasted figure was changing, she could feel it inside. She reminded herself of the fertility goddess statues she had seen in the National Geographic Magazines they would sneak as school kids. Full, plump, lush. Life did not come from scarcity; it was borne of abundance.

Carrying her water bottle, Cass came around the bend on the path and saw the Ladies Who Lunch sitting at the picnic table. Lauren smiled and waved her over. Frozen in her tracks, Cass weighed her options. It would be futile to pretend she hadn't seen them; she'd already made eye contact with Lauren. She would be lying if she said she had someplace to be, not that they would know any different. Somehow, though, she didn't want any dishonesty in her friendship with Lauren. Cass decided to channel her inner socialite—everybody had one, paste on a big smile, and walk over like she belonged there. Who was to say she didn't?

Apparently, Caroline was the one to say she didn't. Caroline looked directly at Cass, eyes narrowing, mentally daring her to sit down. What is her deal? Cass thought to herself. What did I ever do to her?

Cass decided that this was ridiculous. She was a grown woman. This was not high school, and she would sit wherever she felt like, thank you very much, especially when invited. Choosing the seat directly across from Caroline because that happened to be the one open, she met her glare with a challenge of her own.

"Nice day, hey Caroline?" Cass would force her to be openly ugly to her if that was how she wanted to play it. None of this secret cutting eyes garbage over the heads of the others.

Caroline made an excuse about catching up on some budget paperwork before a meeting that afternoon, cleaned up her lunch, and made a beeline for the building. Without so much as a backwards glance, she strode across the grass, skipping the meandering path altogether, and went back into the cold steel and glass structure. Cass could see a similarity between Caroline and the building.

Never one to miss an opportunity to dig for details, Shelby piped up, "What is her deal?"

"I think *I* am her deal, but I'm not sure why." Cass replied thoughtfully. This pregnancy was maturing her in ways she hadn't anticipated, and the ability, no, the desire, to speak her mind, was one of them. Cass could see herself as a tree finally sending down roots and branching out, instead of a Charlie Brown Christmas tree, sparse and undeniably desperate. "Have I done something to offend her?"

"I think she used to be married and it didn't end well," Shelby began. "Maybe it's the thing you had with Cato. Not that that's any of our business," she said quickly.

Never one to hide from an elephant in the room, Shelby called it like she saw it. Cass's cheeks caught fire as she looked at Lauren for help, wondering how much Shelby actually knew.

"Cass, I'm not judging. I'm just saying. Maybe she doesn't like you because you remind her of something painful. Something she'd rather forget. Maybe," she said, drawing the word out, "maybe *you* should talk to *her.* You know, level the playing field. Force her to show her hand."

"Yeah, I'm not so sure about that."

Breaking her silence, Lauren spoke up. "Shelby, this is not intended for gossip, so don't go getting all excited." It was Shelby's turn to blush. "But, Cass, you should know that Caroline was married at one time, but her husband left her for someone in his office, about four years ago. I imagine that seeing you *is* a painful reminder of what happened in her own life. While this isn't about you, it's about you. Does that make any sense?"

"Tons."

Cass couldn't help but like Shelby for all her directness. She figured the woman to be at least ten years her junior, but was pleased at the possibility of a friendship with her. What a collection they would make. Each covering a different decade, assuming Caroline brought her forty-somethingness back to the party.

Cass relaxed a bit, listening to the small talk between Lauren and Shelby. It was clear that Lauren had a mentor relationship with her, something that appeared to come naturally. Age, wisdom, Cass wasn't sure what exactly it was, but there was definitely something about Lauren that encouraged you to be better than you were, but not in a pretentious way. She held herself to certain standards and others simply fell in line with that. Cass couldn't deny that it happened to her when she was around Lauren. Like a thirsty person to water, Cass was drawn to Lauren. There was safety, peace about her. Shelby seemed to respond to that as well.

Drawing her mind back to the group, Cass listened as they talked about an upcoming event they were all going to. Some sort of girls' night, only they didn't seem to be talking about a club.

"Cass, you should come."

"I'm sorry . . . must have been day dreaming. Come where?"

"For coffee with us. We are going, and by we, I mean Caroline too, if she'll come, meeting at the cafe in Lauren's church for coffee. They make the best cappuccinos, almost as good as the guy at Caffeinated."

"Coffee makes me sick these days," Cass blurted out without thinking. Shelby's eyebrows shot up to the top of her head. Cass tried to cover by studying the butterscotch candy she was unwrapping, saying that she had never tolerated the heat well, even as a child. Lauren shot Shelby a look that clearly said *Leave it alone.*

Cass still wasn't sure she was ready to join the group away from work. Hanging out at the company picnic table was one thing; attending a function, no matter how innocent and laid back, was completely another thing. "Why not just go to a regular coffee shop?"

"It's kind of an event over at the church. They're calling it a Summer Harvest, you know, to gather up with your friends. With everyone so busy in the summer, it is just a chance to sit down, relax, and catch up. No pressure, though. You decide. I've gone to things there before and even though I'm not there every Sunday, it's a nice place to be. Everyone's real down to earth."

"When is it?" Cass asked, still stalling, looking for a graceful way out. It did sound sort of fun though. That tree putting down roots was shaking the ground she walked on, she could feel it. *Putting down roots means turning over soil, disrupting life around you.* Her mouth answered that she would love to go before her brain came up with a reason to back out. Hate it when that happens. Three weeks was time enough to either get used to the idea or move out of town.

Shelby clapped her hands with a squeal, and Cass couldn't help but smile in return. *Who is this baby is making me to be,* she thought. She looked to Lauren, who gave her an encouraging grin.

"You'll have fun. Trust me."

Oddly enough, for having known them for such a short time, she did.

Caroline, however, was another story.

Besides the fact that her clothes were getting a little snug, it had been a while since Cass had treated herself to a new outfit. Walking back into the office with Lauren and Shelby, she decided she would indulge in something summery for the coffee night. She was sure those church-type ladies wore dresses all the time anyway, and didn't want to look like she didn't fit in.

Catching a glimpse of Caroline at the vending machine, Shelby didn't miss the opportunity to tell her the good news. "Hey Caroline, guess what? Cass is joining us over at Lauren's church for the Summer Harvest. Isn't that great?"

Cass couldn't decide if Shelby was pushing either of their buttons, or if that's just the way she was. She chose to err on the side of friendship, believing she was indeed just excited about the night.

"*Really?*" Caroline turned on her heel, Diet Coke in hand, without another word.

Cass was beginning to wonder what she had gotten herself into. She headed back to her own desk and focused on the task at hand. Keeping the company well staffed was her goal;

keeping herself sufficiently distracted was a fringe benefit. Also at work keeping her sufficiently distracted was the need to use the bathroom every hour. Like clockwork, no matter what she'd had to drink. Each trip, Cass could feel the eyes of her co-workers on her. It wouldn't be long before her body gave away her secret altogether.

CHAPTER 12

Five o'clock finally showed up and Caroline shut down her computer, glancing around the office as the computer went through its shutdown cycle. She caught Cass's eye. The two locked up, but to her credit, Caroline thought, Cass did not look away first. Must be a bit of steel in there.

The voice of her therapist echoed in her head as she took measured steps across the office. "Back off, Caroline. Deal with your stuff yourself. This has nothing to do with her." Ignoring the voice of reason, she stood directly over Cass, shiny black hair swinging into her face.

"So. I heard they invited you to coffee. It's at a church you know." The accusation that she didn't belong there hung heavy in the air.

With that, Caroline spun on her heel and clipped her way to the elevator.

Fuming, Cass wondered why she let that woman get to her. She had a way of making her feel like the time she'd shown up for the first day of school with no school supplies or lunch box. Inadequate, defenseless. Ashamed. Cass could feel the roots that had stretched out this morning shrinking back. Get angry, Cass. Don't let her do that to you.

Knowing she was a pawn in a situation that didn't concern her directly did help a bit, but it did not completely restore the excitement of buying a new dress that she was looking forward to. Caroline was a kill joy, that was the best word for her. A bully and a kill joy. Well, I am not going to give her the satisfaction of letting her get to me. With that, Cass fluffed her auburn hair, applied some fresh lipstick, and grabbed her bag. One last trip to the restroom and she was on her way, laughing to herself that the company should add a toilet paper surcharge to her paycheck.

Cass pulled into the parking lot of Colby's, the department store everyone shopped at, judging by how often women were complimenting each other for wearing the same thing they were. She hoped she would find something suitable, something flattering, briefly wishing she had someone with her to offer an opinion. Grabbing a few sun dresses in her size, she headed into the dressing room. She hoped the fullness of the dress would offer a place to keep her stomach.

Pulling the first one over her head, she was shocked at how her breasts had grown. What would have been flattering on a smaller framed woman was somewhat obscene on her, breasts spilling out in all directions. Frustrated, she tried on the second dress, a pretty turquoise shade that flattered her skin tone. The waist was gathered at exactly the wrong spot; there was no way this dress was going below her armpits. What had started out as an adventure was turning into a disaster. She pulled on her work clothes and opened the door to her dressing room stall.

Shelby jumped back with a start and burst out laughing. "We have got to stop meeting like this!"

Seeing the dresses in Cass's hand and the disappointment on her face, she took a chance. "Shopping for something new for Lauren's get together?"

"I thought so, but nothing fits right."

Taking another step, Shelby offered to help her find something. "You know," she began gently, "the boobs show up and your waistline disappears before anything else happens. Not that I ever minded the boobs showing up. I waited a long time to actually need a bra," she laughed, gesturing at her small chest. "My husband always says he doesn't mind flat-chested women, but he sure seemed to take an interest when that changed."

Cass's golden brown eyes narrowed as she debated whether to put Shelby out of her misery or let dig her hole a little deeper. "Ok. You know. It's not like it would've been a secret for much longer anyway."

Shelby rambled on as she lead Cass to a different set of dress racks, helping her choose a few selections with empire waists. "The nice thing about these is that they gather in higher up, not right at your natural waist. You'll be able to wear these for awhile, and then again after, depending on when your baby is due. I'm still waiting to fit into my clothes I wore B.C. Before children," she elaborated, seeing the curious look on Cass's face.

Cass enjoyed the feeling of camaraderie she experienced with Shelby. Being pregnant was new to her, and it was good to have someone to share it with, even if she was considerably younger than her. The pregnancy closed the gap and almost made them peers.

"The doctor says late January or so. First babies are always late, but since this I am a bit older than the average first time mom, we'll play it by ear. But yes, I don't think I'll be hauling out the bikini next summer," she laughed, enjoying the easy rapport.

Shelby insisted she pick out a pretty necklace to match the deep bronze colored dress. She felt almost elegant in the dress, sexy even, like she imagined a mother earth type feeling. Despite all the changes going on in her body, she felt comfortable in her skin in a way she never had. New sandals completed the look. Cass found herself looking forward to the night she would wear her new outfit.

"When you are ready to bust into maternity wear, no pun intended, let me know. I'd be happy to shop with you." Cass promised to take her up on the offer.

Famished after the long day, Cass stopped at the convenience store near her house for a salad. It was probably two clicks healthier than a burger, she thought, looking at the smothering of bacon, cheese, and hardboiled egg. "Hey, at least it's a salad," she complimented herself. She recognized the attendant as the man who usually worked the early morning shift, and wondered what he was doing there so late in the day, asking him as much.

"With privilege comes responsibility," he joked lightly. "The weather's nice and my afternoon kid wanted to go to the beach, so I'm filling in. No biggie. I get to see the regulars coming and going."

Taking her salad, Cass felt a strange sensation in her belly. She stopped short, but it was gone. Must be a bubble, she thought to herself. A hunger pang. She drove home, eager to dive into her dinner.

It's at a church, you know.

The words hung heavy in the air, the echo replaying in Cass's mind like a playground taunt. It was like Caroline knew she wouldn't be comfortable there. She didn't even own a Bible. The one at home had weighed about sixteen pounds and functioned as a flower press, obituary saver, and stand for a cute little figurine her mother had. Every respectable house had a Bible, so Geri made sure they had a nice big one, but Cass had never gotten around to buying one for her apartment.

Cass resolved to pick one up before the coffee night.

Stopping off at the bookstore closest to the office, she asked directions to the Bible section, feeling like she had two heads from the look the clerk gave her. She followed the directions and found herself staring at two full cases of Bibles. Seriously? This was going to be harder than she thought, but she wasn't going to give Caroline the last laugh.

She picked up a smaller model of the one she had at home . . . King James Version. Black binding. Foreboding. She let it fall open and read "Thou wilt keep him in perfect peace, whose mind is stayed on thee."

The meaning was lost in the *thee's* and *thou's*, although she was intrigued by the peace part. She slid that Bible back on the shelf and began searching in earnest.

Reference Bibles, Study Bibles, Children's Bibles, Archaeological Bibles, Hebrew Bibles . . . And then there were the different translations. King James, now she had heard of that one. New King James? What happened to the old King James?

New Living Translation, NIV, TNIV, RSV, NRSV, the Message, New American Standard, the list went on. Feeling flushed and out of place, Cass started back towards the door, when the shelf tag Women's Bibles caught her eye. They were lighter and more casual looking than the black leather-bound ones, but she figured the words had to be the same, right?

A Devotional Bible for Mothers, the binding said. She reached for it, afraid of what it might feel like in her hand. It had weight, but not in an overwhelming way. She let the pages fall apart, reading the page that opened. There was a small message about the text, with some words of encouragement to the reader. "As you shepherd your children, let the Lord shepherd you." Psalm 23 was next to that, and as Cass read, something familiar began to resonate within her. She remembered these verses from a funeral she'd attended as a teenager, but these words did not speak of death. These words spoke of safety and comfort, of peace. She never knew that the Bible was meant to bring comfort and peace. She was sure the Bible would point out her problems and shortcomings, and remind her of all the ways she had failed.

A shepherd for life. For my life, Cass thought, as I will shepherd my child, Jesus will shepherd me. Shepherds don't scream and condemn. Shepherds lead and protect.

For the first time, Cass wondered if she really had misunderstood who Jesus was and what He wanted from her. She wondered if there might be a place for her in His world.

Cass closed the Bible and carried it to the front. She hoped the clerk wouldn't think she was some kind of zealot or religious nut, buying a Bible. Who did that? She laid the book on the counter, one hand lingering close by, afraid to let it out of her possession completely. She knew that somehow, this book was going to change her life. She could feel it. The taunting of Caroline ceased to matter. Actually, she realized that without it, she would not have come shopping in the first place.

CHAPTER 13

Please, please, let me have an umbrella in my car. Cass wasn't sure that she'd replaced her umbrella since totaling her car. Low dark clouds broke up the pleasurable monotony of blue skies and warm temperatures, promising stormy weather before the day was through.

Not finding an umbrella, Cass searched the lot for a parking spot close to the building and came in a different entrance, missing the police cruiser parked directly in front of the building.

Stepping off the elevator, she wondered at the commotion around the reception desk as she approached her work station.

"We don't have a *Sandy* Parker here," she heard Claudia insist to two uniformed officers. "You're sure that's the name?"

Cass blinked several times in rapid succession, certain she had misunderstood.

"Sandy is the first name, yes." The officer confirmed.

Aware her composure was fleeing the scene, Cass walked on rubbery legs towards the officers. She could see the shorter officer, Troy, his badge said, holding a backpack, and came closer to see what was going on.

"Um," Cass began, swallowing past the small bird that had taken up residence in her throat suddenly, "Y-you were looking for a Sandy Parker? Who is looking for her?"

"We need to talk to her directly. Do you know where we can find her?"

Not meeting anyone's curious glances, Cass motioned them aside. "The only person who called me Sandy was my father, but I haven't seen him since I was seven years old. No one has heard from him in over twenty-five years."

"Ma'am, what was your father's name?"

"Landry Alan Parker. People called him Lan for short."

"Ma'am, would you like to step into a conference room or someplace more private? We need to talk to you."

Cass could feel the eyes of a small crowd watching her as she made her way down the hall, albeit unsteadily. She led them to a small conference room and the taller of the officers, his badge identifying him as Taylor, drew the blinds.

Lauren and Shelby glanced at one another, each mirroring the other's expression of furrowed brow and concern. Lauren took a step towards the conference room but hesitated; she would be ready when Cass came out.

"Ma'am, we know this isn't what you thought you were going to hear today. We have this backpack we believe belonged to Landry Alan Parker."

The other officer took over the conversation. Wryly, Cass wondered, if they would fall into a good cop/bad cop routine. She wasn't sure what she would need to be bad copped about.

HE KNOWS YOUR NAME

"Ma'am . . ."

"Call me Cass."

"Cass, we found this backpack in a car, along with the body of Mr. Parker, in February. It appears that he was living in the car and succumbed to the cold. Along with the backpack were empty soup cans and boxes of cereal. Ma'am . . . Cass, we are very sorry for your loss."

"The backpack was the only thing of value in the Ford Fairlane. We found a luggage tag attached to it, this one here," he said pointing to a tag. "Inside the tag was a note reading *'Please deliver to Sandy Parker if found'*. We were able to trace you through records containing your father's name and your birth certificate."

"Ma'am, what would you like us to do with this?" he asked, holding the backpack towards her.

Cass's knees deserted her as she sat heavily in the chair. With shaking hands, she reached for the backpack. What probably used to be light blue had changed to sooty gray over time. As she touched it, she realized this was the first time she had held something that had been in her father's hands in over twenty-five years. She wanted to hold it, feel for some lingering warmth, some evidence that he had existed.

The officers had her sign a few release documents and left her with the backpack and some paperwork identifying the location of her father's grave. Cass set the filthy pack in a chair opposite her and stared at it for a long minute. It seemed to possess a life of its own, but that would be silly. Backpacks don't breathe.

She knew she wouldn't look in it that day.

A gentle tap at the door revealed Lauren's concerned expression.

"It's my dad's," Cass said numbly. "He's dead." She couldn't bring herself to share any details of where and how he died.

Cass knew there should be sadness, relief, vindication, joy, *something* going on, but all she felt was flat.

"It's the only thing I have of my dad's, and I don't know what to do with it."

"Do you want to open it? I'll sit with you while you do," Lauren offered.

Although grateful for the older woman's compassion, Cass declined the offer. She was not ready to deal with whatever secrets the backpack might reveal. It was easier to hate him as an inanimate object, the way one hates all furniture reminiscent of the home they grew up in, than to actually open the pack and have to see him as a real person with real possessions.

Even *if* that lifetime was contained in a smelly, sooty backpack.

Leaning forward with her head on her hands, she let out a deep breath. Do not break down right here. Do *not* break down right here. Don't give anyone the satisfaction of seeing you come out of yet another meeting all blotchy faced and puffy eyed. Let the tongues wag and the gossips wonder, but God, please give me dignity. If You are up there, please do this one thing for me.

Taking a deep breath, she slid the rolling chair out behind her and slowly came to her feet. The constant nausea compounded by the shock of learning her father was dead left her light-headed, and Lauren was quick to take her arm, steadying her as she got her sea legs. *This was walking into unknown territory*, Cass thought. *Up until now, it was easy to wish him dead. Did I cause this? Was there something I could have done? Does my mom know?* The questions came quicker than the answers that afternoon.

"Let's get this to your car before the rain hits." Lauren motioned to take the backpack for Cass, lifting it by the handle at her assent. She wasn't ready to feel the pulse it contained again. Cass went to her desk to grab her keys and a butterscotch.

The wind whipped their hair into their eyes, the burst of cold carried on the steamy air announcing the approaching front. Lauren set the backpack in her backseat, but at Cass's direction relocated it to the trunk. She didn't want to see it looking at her as she drove. Truth be told, she didn't actually want it in her car. She was hauling enough baggage around, although invisible, and didn't want to add to the clutter.

She declined an offer to take the rest of the day, knowing that nothing productive would come of it anyway. With a baby on the way, she needed to make every hour count.

"I'll sort through it on maternity leave," she told Lauren.

"That's not until January, Cass."

"I know," she said firmly, ending all further discussion.

Maternity leave. She was going to be a mom, and now her baby really had a grandfather, even though he was a dead one. At least that beats a missing in action one.

As she reached to slam the trunk, her hand behaved of its own accord, unzipping a side pocket on the grungy backpack. Little yellow wrappers fluttered about as the breeze caught them. Butterscotch candy wrappers. Cass pulled her hand back like she'd been burned.

Lauren looked at her in surprise. "Did you know he liked those?"

Cass shook her head quickly, not wanting to find any kinship with him. A picture began to form in her mind . . . Lan reaching his hand to an inside pocket always stocked with butterscotch candies, handing one to her too, despite her mother's objections.

"That girl is going to choke to death and it will be all your fault, Landry."

Cass couldn't have been more than five at the time, and today would have agreed with her mother's assessment. Small kids shouldn't have hard candy. They'll choke. Said so right in the manuals she'd been reading. In that minute, something like familiarity began to grow, a shared history that had been long suppressed.

Swallowing hard, she closed the trunk and ducked low, scurrying back to the office as the first heavy drops began to fall; she committed to getting ten background checks done from the growing pile of resumes on her desk before the day's end.

She exhaled deeply, steeled herself against the questioning glances that awaited her, and walked directly into the ladies room to deal with the churning in her stomach.

Something's got to give.

Arriving home that afternoon, windshield wipers doing double duty, Cass popped the trunk and grabbed the pack before she changed her mind. She'd battled an irrational thought all day that she'd locked her dad in her trunk, not an inanimate object, and resolved to at least bring the poor guy into the house.

Really, she told herself, it's a bag of stuff. Just a bag of stuff.

She grasped the handle, knowing that at least at some point in the last six months, her dad's hand had touched the same spot. *Weird.* Really, there was nothing about this situation that wasn't weird. Her dad froze in his car. Why didn't he go someplace? What had happened to him since she last saw him? If anything, Cass knew the answers she sought might be in that pack.

She carried the pack in the house and set it in the corner opposite the couch. Cass hoped no smells were going to leak from the bag and into her house. God knew, the last thing she needed was something stinky to upset her stomach. Foot raised, she resisted the urge to kick the back pack.

How dare he show up here, unannounced, into my life. She was just getting settled with the idea of a baby, and rebuilding the relationship with her mom. The last thing she needed was drama. She'd had enough of that to last a life time.

Kicking up the air conditioner a notch to dispel the July humidity, she fixed herself a glass of sweet tea and perched on the edge of the couch to survey the small piece of luggage from a safe distance. Emotions tumbled, each vying for a voice and expression.

"Well, dad, welcome to my house. I'm sure you'll be quite comfortable here." She spoke into the air, feeling foolish but not knowing what else to do. Cass thought about calling her mom, but knew she needed time to process this turn of events on her own.

With a sob that came out of nowhere, Cass's anguish broke the surface. Alone in his car. Oh dad, why? Why? I could have helped you.

Cass found herself on her knees in front of the backpack, cradling it to herself, as the tears cascaded down her cheeks. Rocking it like an inconsolable infant, she cried the tears of a child abandoned all over again. "Dad. Dad."

Memories of tears cried in her bed, crying "Daddy, Daddy" overwhelmed her. She thought the feelings she'd had for her father were dormant, but tonight they woke, the backpack a key unlocking something raw, something primeval in her. No child gets over losing a parent, no matter what the relationship. Cass realized that she would grieve for this man, this man who gave her life but lost his own, cold and alone. She was not prepared for the grief, the guilt that overtook her.

The wind and rain battered the windows, providing a backdrop that mirrored the emotion of the day.

She lifted the backpack gently, reverently, and set it on the couch, wrapping a blanket around it much the way someone tucks in a child. She turned off the light in the living room and went to bed, exhausted tears flowing again. "Oh, Daddy," she sobbed, broken that the chance to know her father was officially over.

Across town, Caroline sat in the dark before a blinking cursor, looking at the name on the computer screen.

Cato Johnson.

Had to be the same one. How many Cato's were out there? This one claimed his residence as a town in Ohio. How had he gotten settled elsewhere so quickly? Only one way to find out, Caroline thought as she reached for her phone.

After all, a man deserves to know he's about to be a father.

As she double checked the number on the screen, a shrill ring filled the air. She glanced down, startled.

Her mother.

Caroline waited until the last possible second to answer, clicking the button and holding the phone to her ear without speaking.

"Caroline? Caroline, I know you're there. I heard you pick up."

"What do you want?"

"I'd hoped we'd moved on, but I see we haven't. Caroline, it's your father. He's not well." Caroline could picture her perfectly coiffed mother, eyebrows arched in a show of dismay as she spoke. "He was diagnosed with bone cancer in April. We didn't want to bother you, but he is not responding well to the treatment. Caroline, he's asking to see you."

A long moment passed as Caroline steadied herself.

"Mother, you may tell him to rot in—"

"Caroline!"

She slammed her phone shut and shoved it away from her with such force it clattered across the counter and shattered on the kitchen floor.

"You can both rot for all I care."

CHAPTER 14

Cass woke before her alarm and fixed herself a cup of peppermint tea. That little life inside her put the cabash on coffee. Just the smell made her gag.

She took her tea to the couch and got under the blanket with the back pack, thinking she must be losing her mind just a bit. Visions of that Castaway movie with Tom Hanks and the volleyball danced across her mind. She figured she was one step ahead of sanity as long as she left the backpack at home during the day, although she did consider leaving the TV on.

Showering and dressing for work, she donned a pair of summery Capri's, drawstring waist tugging at her midsection. Yesterday's storms had given way to milder temperatures and a welcome break in the humidity.

Cass alternated between wanting the whole world to know she was going to be a mom and not wanting to face the curiosity and speculation her condition would certainly generate. Being a single mom wasn't the way she had planned her life, but she made up her mind to enjoy everything about the journey, however it had come about.

"I will be home later, dad. We'll talk then." Her finger traced a trail across the handle.

Cass stopped for a burger, bleu cheese and onion strings on it. Bacon too, just in case the onion strings didn't bring on the heartburn quick enough, she thought sarcastically. Breathing brought on heartburn. Water gave her heartburn. Everything set her throat on fire, so she might as well indulge, Cass figured. Eating sensibly wasn't doing her any favors anyway.

Cass contemplated opening the pack as she munched her burger. Curiosity began to stir the despair. This was her last connection to her father, and as much as she feared what she might find, she couldn't help but wonder how a life lived is contained in one stained backpack. Only able to eat half her burger, she wrapped up the other half for her lunch, knowing the flack she was going to take at the lunch table but deciding it was worth it. Besides, it was nice having people worry and fuss over her for a change.

Cass hugged the pack to her chest, deliberating her next step.

What would Lauren do? Probably pray or something holy like that. Okay. Alright. Here goes.

"Dear God, um, if you can hear me, this is big. I don't know what to do with this backpack. Help. Oh, and um . . . say hi to my dad, if you see him." Feeling silly and not sure anyone was listening on the other side, she quickly said "Amen".

Cass opened her eyes and blinked against the late afternoon sun slanting in her window. Stanley brushed up against the pack, arching his back as he stood on tip toes, the rumbling of a small motor deep within emanating from him.

"What are you so excited about?" she grumbled. "I wasn't talking to you. Fine, I was praying," she explained to the cat that at least had the decency to pretend interest, until a fly buzzing on the window sill stole his attention. "That *better* not have come out of this backpack."

Cass was a little freaked out about the whole praying episode. She wasn't sure what had possessed her to do it, except that she knew Lauren probably would have. Praying indicated a modicum of certainty that one was talking to someone. What if . . . what if there was someone listening?

What would that say about *her*? That she was worth listening to? That possibility hadn't occurred to her before. Knowing, as her father had told her, that he had lost three sons before she was born, she'd grown up feeling like she was taking up space meant for someone else. The runner up. The honorable mention. Oh yeah, this is our daughter. Our consolation prize.

Taking a deep breath, Cass set the backpack on the carpet and unzipped the front compartment. Seemed like the best place to start, at the front. She felt a connection to her father, one that she had waited her whole life to feel.

Unzipping that first zipper, she unearthed an avalanche of butterscotch candy wrappers, Pop-tart crumbs, and other assorted small trash. She emptied the front pocket of a library card, a frequent buyer card for a gas station she wasn't familiar with and a 1962 Cleveland Indians baseball card, some guy named Johnny Romano. Wrapped in a rubber band were business cards of various social workers, shelters, and a voucher from the Salvation Army for a motel room.

Relieved by the trivial nature of what she'd found, she decided to move on to the next compartment. She got up for a drink of ice water and a stretch, reaching her arms to the sky for a moment, working the kinks out. Carrying a growing person inside put a lot of strain on a body, Cass was realizing.

The next zipper stuck a little, and as she worked it open, she found a pair of gloves, some clean socks, a toothbrush and toothpaste, and a small bottle of Aqua Velva. She opened the container and chanced a sniff, and was transported back to a time her mind had forgotten but her heart remembered.

The icy scent slapped on his cheeks. Standing in his undershirt, shaving cream on his face. Cass, Sandy as he called her, sitting on the toilet seat watching her dad shave. He whistled under his breath, through his teeth, as he skillfully guided the blade across his cheeks, his top lip, and on his neck, weaving a trail through the white foam. He never did teach her how to whistle like that. On those days, the house felt different. Happier.

Sitting on the toilet seat, watching Daddy shave and whistle as he slipped her the butterscotch's her mother was sure would lead to certain death, those were the things she missed about her dad when he left.

When times were harder and the butterscotch candy had been replaced by a smoke and a drink, bathroom chats fell by the wayside. The stubble grew, giving him a haunted hollow look. Daddy didn't look friendly then, and he sure didn't whistle. The stains sat on the undershirt, unchanged, and she avoided being in the same room with him. This wasn't the man she wanted to remember, but it was the one who inhabited the majority of the memories.

The butterscotch candy wrappers and the Aqua Velva gave Cass hope that the dad she wanted to remember had found his way back. Maybe the demons he wrestled with had been laid to rest. Something akin to peace began to find its way into the creases of Cass's heart as she grappled with the conflicting emotions that marked her feelings towards her father.

She wanted to continue to hate him for what he had done to their family, but the older she got, the more she realized that everyone is just doing the best they can with what they have.

Being this close to his intimate belongings was oddly comforting. It was safe because these things couldn't hurt her, but it allowed her to see him as a person. A hurting person in need of the same things she was.

Contentment squeaked its way next to Cass as she sat surrounded by the debris of her father's last days. The July sky danced with pink, orange, and smoky gray as night crept closer. Something unfolded in Cass's chest, nothing she could put words to, but she knew things were changing for her.

With shaking hands, she reached for the last zipper. The final frontier, she thought to herself with a grin. Like an astronaut heading into alien territory, she was about to uncover the final secrets of her father's life. Well, maybe not all that, but at least she would see what was in the rest of the back pack. The zipper caught on a thread and threatened to derail. Cass found herself unwilling to risk breaking the zipper altogether, and got up to get a pair of scissors. Rummaging in the drawer by the phone, deep in thought, she jumped a foot when the phone next to her rang.

Seeing that it was her mother, she almost let it ring, but her conscience got the better of her.

"Hi, Mom," she said, trying to muster more enthusiasm than she felt.

"Cass, is everything okay? You sound funny." Geri worried enthusiastically, like it was a sport with a prize. "Everything okay?" she asked again.

"Yes, Mom, fine. We are both doing fine," knowing her mom was concerned about the baby. Cass again considered telling her mom about the backpack but needed to finish her excavation of it first.

She still felt responsible to protect her mom from certain information, but in honest moments, Cass knew it was more about needing to shield *herself* from her mom's reactions than protecting her mom in general. If her mom didn't know about something, Cass wouldn't have to worry how she felt about it and then deal with that. Makes perfect sense. *If you are neurotic*, Cass chided herself. Still, all things considered, she wasn't telling her yet.

"Well, you sound funny. You would tell me if something was wrong, right?"

"Yes, mother. How are you doing? What are you up to on this fine summer evening?"

Glad that her mother had settled down a bit, Cass listened as she told her about the crochet club she had joined. She and her lady friends got together a few mornings each week and made scarves, hats, and mittens for the local elementary school. Occasionally they switched it up and made hats for the cancer center. Mostly it was just an excuse to get together and chat about what was going on in their kids' lives. Cass knew she was the hot topic, and it was about to get hotter once she told her about the backpack. She listened distractedly as her mother prattled on, making the occasional grunt and uh-huh when there was a lull.

"Cass? Cass? Are you even really listening?"

"OK mom, you got me. I am a little sleepy and was getting ready to lie down for a bit," Cass skirted the truth and used the baby card. "Is it okay if I call you later in the week?"

"Alright honey. You take care of yourself and my grand-baby, hear? Talk soon."

Hanging up the phone, Cass grabbed the scissors and snipped the thread impeding her progress. She opened the pack, and reached in, pulling out a gallon sized Ziploc bag. Inside the bag was a book covered in grocery sack, like she used to do when she was in grade school. There were a few envelopes, a pen, and a notebook. Cass opened the sealed bag with shaking hands, letting the book slip from her grasp momentarily.

Faded black and white pictures fluttered gently to the ground. Pictures of her as a baby, pictures of her father as a young man, his arm around a pretty chestnut haired woman Cass recognized as her mother when she was a teenager. There were pictures of him cradling Cass, looking stunned at the fragility of the life he was holding. Somehow, he had pictures of Cass at her sixth grade graduation, wearing that awful dress her mother had made her wear. Looking at it now, though, Cass realized it wasn't awful. And she wasn't ugly. Actually, in that picture, she looked a lot like the prettiest girl in the whole eighth grade. How had she not seen that? And *how* had her dad gotten that picture?

Her senior picture was in the stack, a color picture showing off the highlights she had put in herself for the occasion. A picture of her with her mom and grandmother, Cass in her cap and gown. Dylan and Cass on their wedding day, the same picture she had on the dark paneled wall in that trailer long ago. Seemed like an eternity ago, smoke still curling in the picture like it was just yesterday. Snapshots frozen in time. A whole bag of them.

Cass felt the tremor begin in the pit of her stomach, traveling down to her feet. It's a good thing she was sitting as she could feel her knees sinking into her ankles, the bottom dropping out of what she'd always believed to be true. This did not fit the picture in her mind of her father, a man who vanished from their lives looking for a fresh start. This collection of images did not speak of a man who walked out willingly. Looking at the pictures, Cass could see the fingerprints in the corners made by a man holding all he had left. She gently touched the prints, not wanting them to disappear, but seeking connection with the hands that held them.

The realization that he didn't leave because he wanted to crept towards the edge of her mind, like a deer in the brush. If you turn to look at it, it will bound away, and you will be left wondering if you ever actually saw it in the first place. Cass glanced sideways at the hope waiting in the shadows. She swallowed rapidly, tears stinging her eyes; the first bubbles of joy mingling with regret.

Wiping her nose on the back of her hand, Cass reached for the paper covered book and looked closer at the envelopes, surprised to see her name on one of them.

Gingerly, Cass shook the paper free of the enclosure with her name on it. Sandy. Faded yellow legal pad and blue pen, some of the ink bleeding through, she squinted against her dad's cramped script and the letters blurred over time.

"Dear Sandy,

So many times I thought about picking up the phone, or driving to your mother's house, but I never did. I am learning, at my age, that living with regret is a burden none of us can afford, but some regret is just too heavy to put down. Wishing to do life over again is a waste of time, but if I could, I would. I hold the pictures of you and remember how you felt in my arms that first time I held you. I was so afraid I would drop you or hurt you somehow; you were so tiny, a little rosebud. But boy, could you holler when you needed something.

I don't know what you remember or what your mother told you about me, but I wanted to tell you a few things myself. I know it's too late for you to hear it from me, face to face, but maybe this letter will help. I'm sorry it's all you have.

Whatever I made you feel, no matter how things were explained to you after I was gone, I want you to know that I loved you and your mother. Things did not go as we had planned, and neither of us knew what to do about that. We weren't good for each other, your mother and I, but that shouldn't have been your problem. Hopefully you were too young to remember much, but I know you felt caught in the middle.

Sandy, I hope you grew up strong and brave. I know I never told you, but I'm glad I had a daughter. You were so beautiful, looking just like your mother when she was a girl. Did she ever tell you she was voted the prettiest girl in her eighth grade class? Your grandmother sent me pictures of you when I had an address.

*I never did settle down after your mom and I
split up. I just couldn't seem to put down any roots.
I should have fought harder to stay; I know that
now.*

*If I could have one last conversation with
you, which I suppose this is, I would tell you three
things:*

I'm sorry for the way things ended.

You have never been a disappointment to me.

*Find Jesus. I did and He is the only reason I
made it as long as I did. In the end, it's only about the
grace we accept and the grace we offer others.*

I love you, Sandy.

Dad

*P.S. See you on the other side. I'm saving you a
place right next to me.*

Cass read and reread the letter, wiping her nose on her
sleeve as she didn't trust her legs to carry her to the kitchen
for tissues. All the words she had waited a lifetime to hear. He
loved her. She mattered to him. Happy and sad all at the same
time, she put everything back into the Ziploc bag, including the
letter with Geri's name on it. She just wasn't ready to share
this yet.

Cass jumped at the phone, startled by its shrill ring for the
second time that evening.

"Hello?" she said, voice husky with the effort of holding the
tears back.

"Cass, it's Lauren. Okay if I drop by?"

Cass nodded into the phone, knowing Lauren couldn't hear that. "Uh huh." That woman must have a sort of sixth sense, wanting to chat at a time like this.

Her mind went back to the letter, practically memorized by now; something about it niggled on the edge of her mind. She struggled to bring it into view. She waited for Lauren to tap on her door, knowing she looked a sight.

Lauren had learned over the years not to ignore those little whispers of encouragement to do something. Sometimes it was to drive a certain direction, and she would find someone with a flat tire. Once, she found a guy who'd had a heart attack while riding his bike. Drawing on her first aid training, she was able to do CPR while waiting for an ambulance. When she felt the urge to call and check on Cass, she knew better than to ignore it.

"Mike, I'm going to Cass's. She's had quite the bombshell drop today and I think she could use some company. Or a shoulder."

"Hey, Cass, I hope you don't mind . . ." Her voice trailed off as she saw the contents of the back pack strewn around the room. Looking at Cass for the first time, she caught sight of the bloodshot eyes, blotchy skin, and nose raw from wiping. "Oh honey," she said softly, opening her arms. Cass fell into them, grateful for the older woman's instinct to comfort first and ask questions later.

Sobs quieting, Cass tried to explain. "These are happy tears," she laughed. "He loved me," she said, gesturing for Lauren the letter to read for herself.

CHAPTER 15

"I'm so glad you came with me, Caroline. Gym class was always my worst subject," Shelby said. "But how hard can this be? It's like riding a bike."

The two women each chose a cycle at Fit4You, the gym that collected Shelby's membership dues but not her attendance.

"You're so lucky, tall and thin. I got a new outfit for Lauren's thing and it's a little snug, not that I'll lose anything in two weeks, but maybe I can redistribute what I've got. I can't seem to lose that last bit of baby weight from Trevor, y'know? Can I still call it baby weight if he's six? I mean, technically, it is—"Shelby flushed as Caroline shot her a look that ended all conversation. *Does she ever shut up?*

All business in her bicycle shorts and long-sleeved work-out shirt, she adjusted the seat to fit her long frame and began to pedal slowly, getting a feel for the tension.

"Caroline, wait for daddy. He'll go for a ride with you." *Caroline lifted her face to the sun, shiny black pigtails tied in pink ribbons, and put her feet on each side of the bike frame as she waited for her father. Finally, no training wheels! The band-aids she sported testified of the hard-won skill.*

The spin instructor took command of the class, directing everyone to imagine they were riding on softly rolling hills. Sun on your back, breeze in your face, pedal at a moderate pace and get loose.

"I'm going to show you a trail Daddy used to ride when he was little. Think you can keep up, Bug?" Bug was his special name for her. *Pigtails flying, Caroline pedaled hard, passing her school and the park where they usually played, determined not to disappoint her father.*

"OK, cyclists, we've left the plateau. Adjust your tension and let's hit the hill standing up. We are headed for Kilimanjaro. Come on! You don't want someone to email their pictures. You want to take your own! Push through it! Keep climbing!"

Caroline pedaled faster, breath coming in short gasps.

"Come on, Bug. We're almost there." Caroline could just see her dad's bike disappear along the trail as it entered the thicket. Cool air replaced the sunny day, and the little girl shivered at the drastic change.*

"Hover over your seats, don't sit! We're still climbing. Grab a drink if you need it and keep going. Feel the music. Put yourself in it and let it carry you. And don't. Stop. Pedaling!"

Shelby glanced over at Caroline as she grabbed her water bottle for a swig. Caroline's eyes were screwed shut, a grimace twisting her features as she pedaled furiously. Sweat poured down her cheeks despite the headband pulling her dark hair off her face.

"Good job, Bug! You did it!" her dad licked his lips as he patted the ground beside him. *"Come here, I have something special to show you. Something just for a big girl."*

"Way to go, class! Turn the knob to the left and take off some tension. Just coast. Enjoy the view and take some snapshots before we begin our descent. Don't forget to hydrate."

Caroline pedaled awkwardly into the driveway, unable to keep up the pace her father set. Her mother beamed at her. "Daddy says you were such a trooper!"

"Yes, ma'am."

"Did you fall? Your pigtails are full of leaves. Well, go get washed up then. Good job, baby!"

The little girl looked from one parent to the other, confusion playing on her delicate features. "We'll have to do this again sometime, right, Bug?"

"Yes, Daddy."

Shelby looked to Caroline for a congratulatory high-five as they coasted into their figurative base-camp, but her friend was still pedaling furiously. Tears mingled with sweat and ran down her cheeks, her breath coming in ragged gasps. "Caroline? Hey, um, we're at the bottom. You okay?"

Caroline's eyes snapped open and she blinked against the light, surprised to see Shelby's concerned face. "Going to shower." She grabbed her towel to mop her face. "See you Monday."

That bastard.

CHAPTER 16

"Cass, you look great! I would say pregnancy agrees with you." The soft lilt of Lauren's faded Virginia accent caressed her Cass's ears like a summer breeze. She had a way of talking that invited you closer.

"I read once that the way to stay in shape is to walk your dog every day, even if you don't have one. I'm up to two miles in the evening, as long as it's not too humid or anything."

"You should walk to Mr. Green Jeans." Shelby chimed in.

"What in the world is Mr. Green Jeans?"

"He's this farmer who sets up a little farm stand this time of year right near that bowling alley on Spring Street. It can't be more than two or three miles from your house, Cass. You can work up to it."

"Ha! By the time I work up to it the harvest will be over."

"Speaking of the harvest, do either of you know if Caroline is going tonight? Not that I care or anything. I was just wondering," Cass finished before she dug her hole any deeper.

"I haven't heard from her all week, but I'll be sure to give her a call later today."

"Cass, I'll pick you up at 6:30. Unless you want to walk . . ."

Cass wondered if Shelby's offer to pick her up was a ploy to make sure she actually went, but was happy to take her up on it. Home from work with just enough time to freshen up, Cass jumped in to a quick shower.

One perk of pregnancy was good hair, Cass thought as she worked the shampoo and conditioner through. Looking down, she anticipated the day when she couldn't see her toes. She could see them today, however, and made a note to save time for a quick coat of polish on her toes. She'd picked up a pale seashell pink to complement the deep bronze of her sun dress. Lots of effort going into this church lady event, she'd considered. *Oh well, not much else is filling my social calendar.*

As much as she was looking forward to the evening, even if Caroline was there, she wasn't looking forward to the questions about her husband. She hoped that the bare ring finger staved off those questions, although she'd noticed women at the doctor's office unable to wear their wedding rings due to swollen fingers.

"It's none of your business" probably wouldn't go over well. She decided on graciously brave. "It's just me and the baby." If questioned further, "We are not together anymore" would have to suffice. "I was sleeping around with a guy who wasn't free and got pregnant the day he dumped me" was sure to bring all conversation to a screeching halt. Cass rehearsed her line, smiling in the mirror looking for just the right combination of innocence and courage.

A quick coat of polish on her toes then on to hair and makeup. Cass hoped the humidity didn't wreak havoc on her waves. Not curly enough to kink up, her hair did the opposite in heat and humidity, hanging limp and lifeless. A dusting with loose powder, a bit of mascara, and some gold tinted lip gloss completed the look. Cass loved the sun-kissed glow that came from her auburn coloring. Not fair like a red-head, her golden tones loved the sun.

Not wanting to be unprepared, Cass watched out her patio window for Shelby. Alternately sitting on the arm of the couch, walking to the window to pull the curtain back, she fidgeted with her ring waiting for Shelby.

Twirling the ring on her right hand, Cass slowly removed it and placed it on her left hand. Not meaning to imply anything that wasn't true, but possibly deterring questions and the awkward silence that would follow, Cass left it there. Stretching her arm out in front of her, fingers pointed up, she figured that it would do the job just fine. Not a giant ring by any means, but enough to throw anyone off the scent. After all, single pregnant women probably don't hang around churches very often.

She convinced herself that the deception was doing them all a favor and continued to pace the room, listening for Shelby's arrival.

She wondered for the fiftieth time that day if Caroline would be joining them. She hadn't been at work in a few days, taking some personal time that was due her. Cass wouldn't have to wonder for much longer.

Caroline was caught by surprise as she glanced at the clock; the last ring of the telephone roused her just as the answering machine picked up.

"Caroline, it's Lauren. Hey, just checking in to see if y'all are still joining us tonight. Look for Shelby and Cass if you don't see me right away. Bye!"

Taking a few days vacation, Caroline spent most of her time slicing neat little checkerboards into her thighs where no one would see. Cass's swelling figure and the happy glow about her ate away at Caroline like carbonic acid, stripping the thin veneer of her sanity away. And choosing alcohol over food made for less than precision work.

Caroline woke to the phone bleary eyed, bloody, hair matted, and head pounding as she took in her surroundings. *How did I get here?*

God, where are you? Wasn't I good enough? What more do you want from me?

Caroline's despair had forged a substitute to focus on, and it was Cass.

"The last thing that woman is going to steal is my friends."

With that, Caroline dragged herself from her bedroom cave to the shower. She would be hard pressed to remember her last one. Judging from the greasy condition of her hair, it had been since the last day she went to work. Five days.

She never noticed the ruby rivulets cascading down her thighs as she let the steaming water flow. Head thrown back, the skin on Caroline's five foot ten inch frame hung skeletal from the lack of nourishment. Jet black hair hung straight to the middle of her back. She couldn't buy a curl. Family lore said there was Native American blood in their veins.

That, with the French ancestry, created a temperament few wanted to engage. Cass has no idea who she's dealing with, Caroline thought to herself. No idea.

"No time for this," Caroline sing-songed, dropping her hair dryer in the garbage. She marched into the kitchen, still naked and dripping from her shower for the scissors. Staring at the mirror without seeing anything, Caroline hacked at her hair.

Each piece carried with it the epitaph of anger as it fell to the ground. Every injustice. Every disappointment. Every heartbreak. Every time . . . Caroline stopped just short of remembering. The act of cutting, cutting anything, brought with it release and control. She was in charge of her body, no matter what anybody else told her.

Holding the scissors close to her scalp, Caroline cut as close as she could without lancing her scalp. "I'm not crazy, for crying out loud," she laughed maniacally. Hair stuck to her wet skin; what didn't stick lay in heaps around her feet. "Hobbit feet," she giggled to herself. "I have hobbit feet." Satisfied with her efforts, Caroline moved to her walk-in closet, leaving a trail of blue black revenge in her wake.

Choosing a deep turquoise tank, silky and light, Caroline slid into some summer white Capri length pants and her strappy black sandals with the polished stone inlay.

From a distance, she was a vision of confident haute couture. Tan, short spiky hair, in shape. Up close, she wore the mask of someone with a tenuous grasp on reality. Haunted eyes ringed by large dark circles, lips dry and chapped from lack of water, hands shaking from the events of the past few days. The makeup she applied did not enhance her features, but instead, highlighted the hollowness of her cheeks and her sunken eyes. The cleansing waters of her shower had washed away the newly forming scabs on her thighs; pink stripes were just beginning to seep through the fabric of her pants. Hair was sticking from odd places, trapped by the clothing now holding it into place. The uneven self-imposed shearing completed the picture of someone just south of sanity.

After a quick glance in the mirror at the reflection she never saw, Caroline grabbed her purse and keys. She would show them.

They would regret inviting Cass Parker to their circle.

CHAPTER 17

Pulling into to the parking lot, Cass took a deep breath and held tightly to her new Bible. "Here goes nothing," she coached herself. "Just be yourself." Shelby never let on that she noticed Cass's discomfort, chattering happily about the summer and her kids.

"My youngest is so sweet. He's getting a little nervous seeing all the school supplies out. He asked if I could home school him, all the way through college. 'Mama', he says, 'Can you home college me some day?' Those conversations help balance the ones when he tells me I am the worst mom ever. Seriously, am I supposed to be happy to find the boys covered head to toe in maxi pads in the front yard? So it doesn't hurt as much when we crash into each other, they tell me. The mailman will never let me live that one down," she laughed.

A medium sized building, the church entrance boasted a dramatic floor to ceiling glass window leading to a cathedral roofline. Large wooden beams supported the archway leading to the door, a tasteful combination of new architecture and tradition. To the left of the parking lot was a small pond with a fountain. A pair of swans swam lazily in the evening sun.

The lot was filling rapidly, women calling greetings to one another as they made their way into the building.

Despite the tranquil setting, warning bells assaulted Cass. She had only been inside of a church a few times, and none of them contained memories she cared to repeat. The sideways glances as a young teenager when she and her mother sought a new beginning, the wedding of an older cousin who "had" to get married, the funeral of her grandmother. Yet here she was, in the company of friends, walking in the front door like she belonged there. No one had stopped her yet.

Music greeted the pair in the foyer as they entered the church. Cass noticed the van with the radio station name in the parking lot as they pulled in. Looking at the logo, Cass remembered the station's slogan from the dirty bus that day Cato had left her. "He knows your name . . . WJSS." Holy Roller music, aka Christian contemporary.

Lauren waved to them from across the foyer; as the pastor's wife, she had certain hostess obligations to fill. The greeter at the door welcomed them, handing them a voucher for a drink from the cafe. Cass looked around, feeling alien, yet strangely okay with it. She knew she was on safe ground. Maybe it was Shelby by her side who talked to everyone, introducing Cass with a smile as her friend from work.

The women received her warmly, complimenting her bronze sun dress. She flashed a grateful smile at Shelby for picking it out.

The room was set in summer southwest sunset colors, deep turquoise, vibrant golds and oranges, like a Grand Canyon sunset, Cass thought. The centerpiece of each table held a blooming cactus. Shelby whispered that at the end of the evening some sort of criteria at each table would determine who got to take the cactus home.

"At least this is a plant I couldn't kill," she joked. "They thrive on being ignored."

Cass saw the line forming at the coffee bar and scanned the menu board, deciding on a key lime cooler. She wasn't sure what it was exactly, but it wasn't coffee and it would refresh her. The name practically oozed a cool breeze.

"Hello! Hello everyone!" Their attention was drawn to a woman with a basket holding a microphone. "Welcome to our little get together! While you are waiting to get a drink from the café, take a minute and fill out the welcome card at your table. You'll find a few questions to get the conversations started! Enjoy your evening . . . and no calling home. Your husbands can handle things for a couple of hours." Nods and laughter filled the room. "Don't forget to put your cards in the basket. You never know what surprises are in store for tonight!"

Lauren was just winding down her hostess duties as the line of women entering slowed to a trickle. She took her place in line with them.

"Cass, you look just beautiful! That color brings out the gold highlights in your skin tone. Pregnancy suits you; I always had a tinge of green right up until the day I delivered. Nothing you can wear complements olive green skin," she laughed. "Shelby, did you save us a seat?"

"Right over . . . OH MY . . ."

"Lauren! I made it!"

A stunned silence descended on the room. Women froze in their tracks, and all eyes settled on Caroline.

Tufts of hair poked out of her bra straps and around the straps of her sandals. Her short choppy hair, the glazed look, and the sunken cheeks barely competed with the blood soaking through the thigh portion of her white pants. Her bare upper arms revealed the scars traversing her biceps, normally hidden under sleeves and jackets.

"Caroline! What have you done?" Shelby exclaimed, never one to hold back. "To your hair, I mean. Did you get it cut?" she asked, quickly trying to mitigate her shocked response to Caroline's appearance.

She ran a quaking hand through her jet black spikes. "I didn't feel like drying it so I cut it."

Caroline turned to face Cass head on. "How about you, princess? Want a hair cut? I'm sure we can do something with that." The venom in her eyes knocked Cass in the gut as strong as any physical contact would have. All eyes in the room were on them. She took a step towards Cass. "You think you can have everything you want? Somebody needs to pay. Somebody needs to pay," her voice rose shrilly.

Lauren placed her body between Cass and Caroline, shielding Cass from the threats. Shelby linked arms with her, drawing her closer and forcing her to break eye contact with Caroline, who, because of her height, was able to stare down Cass despite Lauren being between them.

The commotion drew Lauren's husband, Pastor Mike, out of his office. He had met Caroline a few times and had pegged her for a ticking time bomb. He considered it somewhat of a blessing that the bomb blew in his church foyer. With his training in pastoral counseling, he had some resources for diffusing a situation such as this.

The first step was to make sure everyone was safe. Motioning to Shelby to lead Cass to a table, he nodded for Lauren to take a place next to Caroline, instead of directly in front of her. Staying directly in front of an extremely agitated person is a direct threat, a posture of confrontation. Standing shoulder to shoulder with someone brings camaraderie. Whatever was going on with Caroline, she needed to feel secure, not threatened.

Pastor Mike, as she knew him, spoke softly to her, complimenting her hair cut. The blood stains on her pants didn't seem to be from an active wound; he was confident that they were dealing with a psychotic break of some sort. Whether or not it actually involved Cass was yet to be determined, but in his experience, she was simply the catalyst of something that was already brewing.

"Caroline, Lauren, let's take a walk to my office, shall we? We can sit down and sort this out. Have something cool to drink."

Caroline spun to her left and shoved Pastor Mike, her height giving her a benefit that he didn't anticipate. He took a hard step backwards but managed to regain his balance. Caroline took advantage of the opening and raced for the door, screaming obscenities as she went.

That feral smile, teeth bared through pulled back lips, played on her face as she ran headlong through the plate glass window, the one Cass had just admired seemingly a lifetime ago.

The music continued to play and Cass, looking for something to focus on, began to listen to the lyrics. They spoke of a God so powerful He knew the stars by name, but yet the melody invited worship. "Indescribable . . ." What kind of music was this?

Blood pulsed through Caroline's wounds as she laid thrashing on the floor. The intensity of the pain and the noise broke something within her. She pulled her feet to her chest and lay curled in a fetal position, rocking as an eerie high-pitched keening sound emanated from her lips. She was unaware that the noise assaulting her ears was coming from her.

"Someone call 911!" Lauren raced to her side.

A nurse in the crowd came forward to provide medical care. Directing someone to get towels from the kitchen, she applied pressure to the worst of the wounds herself, instructing Lauren to cover the smaller gashes.

Some of the women began to pray for Caroline, that God would provide the healing and peace that she so obviously needed. A young woman with jeans and a summery t-shirt stood, raising her hands. "Oh God," she prayed aloud, "You are Jehovah Rapha, the God who heals. Lord, please draw this broken soul to you. Please calm her heart. Oh God, please help her." She continued to pray aloud as some began to sing and others just stood quietly, holding each another's hands in comfort.

Cass, the object of Caroline's wrath, sat heavily in a chair. Suddenly light-headed from the near physical attack, she instinctively tried to put her head between her knees, but had to settle for her head in her hands but for the baby bump.

Through the crowd, Cass could see Lauren kneeling over Catherine, giving no thought to the blood staining her own clothes. She was whispering to her. Cass couldn't hear what she was saying but the keening and rocking subsided as Lauren continued.

Sirens, faint at first, then louder, announced the arrival of the ambulance. Two young men and a woman came through the door, and, as she surveyed the situation, dispatched the men to bring in the gurney. The woman sat where Caroline could see her and asked her what had happened.

"I—I . . . ran through the glass." She spoke from a place far away, her voice small and distant amid all the commotion. Caroline sounded as shocked to be saying the words as the rest of the crowd was to have seen her do it.

"Let's take a look."

Conversing with the nurse on the scene, she thanked her for her quick actions. "Most of the wounds are surface, but this one, the one you clamped down on, could have done some serious damage."

"Caroline, can you hear me? Caroline?" Quickly lifting her feet into the air, the men lifted her onto the gurney, keeping her feet raised above her head. Shock was a very real possibility in situations of extreme trauma or duress, and this certainly met all the requirements for both.

Caroline's eyes fluttered open as they wheeled her to the waiting ambulance, her turquoise blouse all but unrecognizable.

"Blue and red really do make purple," Cass whispered to herself.

Caroline shifted slightly as they raised the rolling wheels, and seemed to be scanning the room. Cass couldn't be sure, but she was almost certain she saw regret in Caroline's eyes as they met briefly.

Lauren conferred with her husband briefly, then addressed the driver. Running over to Cass and Shelby, she told them she thought she should ride with Caroline.

"Cass, I'm so sorry. Never in a million years could I have anticipated a scene like this one. I don't know what is going on, but I think it best that I go with her. You two stay, ok? For all the mania and aggressive behavior, inside she is probably terrified. I don't want her to go through this by herself. Cass, we will do this again, ok?" she said with a shaky smile. "Well, not exactly this."

Shelby reached out to hug Lauren, saying "Give this to Caroline for me, ok? Keep us in the loop if you can."

The sirens faded into the distance as the murmuring in the gathering of women grew. Stories of hurting relatives, hard times, speculation as to what set her off, many topics besides the summery chit-chat they'd planned for.

Pastor Mike flashed the lights then spoke up.

"Ladies, we have witnessed something troubling and heartbreaking tonight. Join me in a word of prayer, please. 'Father God, You know all things. Please bring help and healing for this woman. Help her to know she is loved by You, first and foremost, and send friends to walk with her during this time. We turn her over to Your care, asking You to shelter and protect her. In Jesus' Name, Amen.' Ladies, I invite you to stay and enjoy your evening of fellowship. I know the fine team who planned this is still looking forward to giving away some prizes. Please keep this woman in your prayers, but *not* your conversations," he said pointedly, knowing a bunch of women together have great power in their conversations, and not all of it good. "Good night everybody; see you Sunday."

"So, what do you want to do?" Shelby inquired of Cass. "This is not exactly how I saw the night playing out."

"Uh, no. Me neither. I wish I knew what set her off or where all this was coming from. You know I just don't have the best luck coming into churches. Something always seems to go wrong."

"I'm sorry, Cass." She paused, considering their options. "Tell you what. I can hear some little desserty things calling my name from that table over there. Let's fix us a plate, hang out for a bit, and take it from there. If you want to leave and go someplace else to talk we can, otherwise, you look beautiful, I am not home with my kids, and we already paid for our drinks. I say we hang around for a little bit, ok?"

Cass nodded her head and followed Shelby to the snack table. She chose a cupcake too adorable to actually eat. Lime green frosting with pink sprinkles. Not really having much of an appetite after the scene with Caroline, she put a few strawberries on her plate next to the cupcake.

Cass waited for the women in attendance to look her way, certain she was on everyone's mind. Sitting with Shelby, feeling for all the world like an outsider, she pulled her wrap tight around her shoulders, thankful she'd thought to grab one at the last minute. Big buildings can be over air-conditioned and she didn't want to freeze.

She waited for the whispers and sidelong glances to begin, and she didn't have to wait for long. Listening to Shelby prattling on about something her son said, Cass began to think of a graceful way to exit this evening.

"He says he can't wait until the new furniture comes because he will bounce even higher when he jumps on it. Seriously, I told him, don't even think about jumping on my new couch. Mommy waited twelve years to get a new one, and it will be twelve more before I get another one. So, do you know what you are having yet? I think girls are easier when they are younger, but you pay for it in the teenage years. Boys, they give it to you all up front. They keep you on your toes, that's for sure."

"Huh?"

"Cass, did you hear anything I just said?"

"What? Oh, I'm sorry. I guess I'm still a little shocked by Caroline. I don't even know what to make of any of it. What does someone need to pay for? She's whispered things to me before about not getting away with anything. Not to sound paranoid, but I feel like she's got it out for me."

"Look, Cass, I know a little bit about her, but I don't want to speak out of turn. She has had some tough times and I'm not sure how well she's dealt with them. From the looks of things, not at all. I can't believe she cut her hair off. She is going to be ticked when she realizes it."

As Cass listened to Shelby talk, she noticed that a few of the women were glancing her way. She dropped her eyes in response, not sure what to do. One of the women, thirtyish with short cropped hair, strolled close to Cass's seat, kept walking, then turned around and came to stand at their table. Cass braced herself for the invitation to take her troubles elsewhere.

"Hey, Shelby." Turning her attention to Cass, she said, "I'm Marcie. I just wanted to say that I'm sorry for the trouble you had tonight. I noticed your dress when you came in and wanted to compliment you on it. I haven't seen you here before, but I hope you come back."

Before she finished, another woman approached their table, emboldened by Marcie, apparently. "You know, I once went to a dinner at my son's school and dumped a plate of spaghetti on the principal's lap. I know it's not exactly the same thing." She faltered in her conversation, face coloring. "I'm just wanting you to know that I understand feeling like everyone in the room is looking at you. Even though we are, we're not." She laughed nervously again. "When you are ready, this is a place you can come back to."

A few more women stopped by with words of welcome and encouragement. Cass would have preferred anonymity overall for the evening, but in light of the way things had gone, this was better than judgment. Cass wondered to herself about a church like this. *Brooke Besor,* the big sign in the parking lot said. She would have to ask Lauren about that.

"So, what do you think? Do you want to leave or hang out for a bit longer?"

"I think I am ready to go; this night has been exhausting. Lots to think about."

CHAPTER 18

The siren blasted through the calm of the summer night. Caroline listened, detached, knowing it had something to do with her. She fought to stay cocooned in the safety of her cottony awareness, a place she didn't have to know anything.

The surface was breaking far over head, the light coming through, but with the light, knowledge. Knowledge that she didn't want to own.

The leather belt buckled firmly against her midsection kept her from curling up, and she felt exposed, stretched out on the gurney unable to protect herself. The wailing continued, intruding into the white space Caroline wanted to melt into. Billowy clouds, gray and soft, beckoned, but she couldn't reach the safety anymore. She became aware of others in the ambulance, including Lauren.

"What is Lauren doing here?" she wondered fuzzily. Craning her head, she took in her surroundings. She was moving. That siren was part of the scene. Everything stung, her arms, her neck, her cheeks; she remembered being clawed by a mama cat once. Was she clawed by a cat?

Like rewinding a VHS tape, the events began to play backwards at high speed. She'd run through that glass window at Lauren's church. She'd pushed Pastor Mike. Oh my God, help me. I pushed Pastor Mike? The black rage put me in front of Cass, and I wanted nothing more than to destroy her. My hair . . . I'm itchy—where is my hair?

Struggling against the restraints, she tried to reach her hair. "Where's my hair? What happened to my hair?" she screamed to no one in particular, knowing she was the only one who could answer that question. She could feel the itch against her skin, like when you get a haircut and no one remembers to dust your back with baby powder. She felt it on her whole body, like bugs crawling on her. "I can't feel my hair! Where is it?"

Lauren met the eyes of the ambulance attendant as he reached for a syringe. Orders had been given to sedate her if she became agitated, and this definitely qualified.

The cotton enveloped Caroline once again, safe, protected, where nothing could hurt her again. She looked dully at Lauren, wondering at the tears on her cheeks of her friend. "What have I done?" she wondered from a place no one could reach.

The ambulance pulled into the emergency room entrance and Caroline's gurney was wheeled into a waiting bay. She was dimly aware of warm water on her body and giggled, hoping she wouldn't wet herself like the old slumber party game they used to play. A stinging followed, then a dull circular pulling on her right shoulder and forearm. Stitches.

Caroline could smell the unmistakable antiseptic scent of the hospital and tried to focus her sight on the large orange flowers that decorated the curtain of her bay in the emergency room. Like big poppies. Poppies made Dorothy sleepy. Her mind had trouble keeping up with her surroundings.

"Ms. McKay? Can you hear me? I'm Dr. Blue. Ms. McKay? Do you remember what happened tonight?"

The eyes of an animal in a trap met the doctor's as she struggled against the knowledge of what she'd done. If I could hold my breath longer, Caroline thought to herself, I wouldn't have to come up. The air on the surface is just too painful to breathe right now.

"We are going to bring you to a private room upstairs, a place where you will be safe. We would like to help you sort through what's going on, okay?"

The doctor's face swam in front of Caroline. "Lauren? You look younger."

"I'm over her, Caroline." Lauren spoke up softly. "What is it?"

"Should I stay?"

Lauren nodded her agreement with the doctor's assessment.

Laying her head back, Caroline didn't argue. She was too exhausted to fight anymore. She just wanted them to let her sleep. Forever.

Caroline didn't open her eyes again until the elevator stopped and she was asked to help them transfer her to another bed. Suddenly very weak, she was unable to cooperate fully and allowed the attendants to do the bulk of the work.

As the nurse settled Caroline into her bed, Dr. Blue motioned for Lauren to follow her.

"I'm Savannah Blue," she said, extending her slim hand. Shoulder length blonde hair pulled back in a pony tail and blue jeans instead of the traditional white jacket were part of her calculated effort to keep patients at ease. "I'm on duty tonight on the MHS floor. Mental Health Services. I got some of the details of what transpired from the driver. Now that her physical wounds are attended to, we will focus on what is really going on."

"Thank you, doctor. I have never seen her do anything like this before."

"We are going to give her something to help her sleep for awhile. In my professional opinion," Dr. Blue said, "she hasn't had solid sleep for at least five days. She appears to have experienced a break at some point. Sleep deprivation brings on psychosis even in quote normal people, but we need to get her some rest to see what drove it in the first place."

Lauren feared for her friend, having her own suspicions what Caroline was running from but no confirmation of that. "Doctor, if there is anything I can do to help, let me know. We've been friends for a few years but Caroline is a pretty private person."

"We need her consent to involve you in any treatment she may agree to. We have strict privacy guidelines for mental health, which sometimes work against us, but we will talk with her tomorrow. Please leave your contact information with the intake nurse, alright?"

Lauren nodded, watching the nurse take Caroline's blood pressure and temperature, checking for any underlying physical conditions.

Certain that Caroline was receiving the best care possible, she provided the information requested. She realized that she didn't have a way home since she rode in the ambulance with Caroline. Funny how details slip your mind in an emergency.

Lauren took Caroline's keys from her purse, intending to drive her car back to her complex. Maybe she would check out her apartment to see if any clues could help the doctor piece together the last five days.

She rode the elevator down to the lobby and went to the sidewalk for better cell phone reception to call her husband, surprised to see Mike's car already there, waiting for her.

"You are a good man, Michael Downs," she said, collapsing in the passenger seat. Exactly ten seconds passed before the tears started, the evening draining her of all emotional reserves. "I don't know what she's dealing with, Mike, but she was barely lucid. It's like she doesn't want to come back."

CHAPTER 19

"I don't know why my mother never did anything."

"Is it possible she didn't know?" Dr. Blue asked.

Caroline took a deep breath, pulling her navy velour robe tight against her. Lauren was so sweet to pick up her things from her apartment, saying nothing about the carnage she had surely seen. The hospital seemed less sterile, less institutional, when she could wear her own clothes, even though they hung on her too thin frame right now. Lauren had even arranged for a friend from church to come in and fix the damage she'd done to her hair.

"I don't know. A mom should just know, right? How does a mother not know that her daughter is being molested in her own house? How does a mother not know?" she said softly into the air. "I tried to tell her once, when I was about eight."

"What happened?" the doctor coached.

"She told me things like that don't happen in families like ours. I must have imagined it or been watching television shows that I wasn't supposed to be. She actually yelled at me for even saying something like that, like it was my fault."

"He always told me I was the special one, like I was supposed to like it or something. I've always been competitive, and as sick as it sounds, even though I knew this was not right,

129

I felt like I won something over my sister. I got to be the special one," voice cracking as she struggled to maintain control. "How could he? Sick bastard. I hate him."

"Caroline, talk to me about what's been going on the last few months. Why do you think this is coming up now?"

Caroline and Dr. Blue processed the events of the last few months together; it was the perfect storm. The anniversary of her husband's walking out combined with the affair she witnessed between her colleagues stirred up feelings of jealousy and abandonment. The spin class was the last straw.

"Caroline, our bodies remember things that our brains are unable to process completely. For some reason, the exercise bike brought you back to the place of remembering that first time. It acted as a catalyst for you, something that speeds up an action already taking place. The increase in cutting tells me that you were on the verge of a breakdown, or breakthrough, depending on how you look at it. This hurts right now, but until we can clean the wound, it will not heal. Does that make sense?"

Caroline continued to stare steadily out the window but never stopped listening. She knew she was right, however painful the journey would be.

CHAPTER 20

Checking the clock in the corner of her computer screen for roughly the nineteenth time that afternoon, Cass couldn't believe it would only be another hour before she would see her baby face to face. Well, screen to face. The desire to know the sex of the baby was pressing in as she reconsidered her decision to keep it a surprise. Maybe she could find out, but keep it a secret from everyone else. She knew she would start shopping like a madman in the appropriate colors though and blow the finale.

Making one last stop at the restroom, she chatted with Lauren on her way out. Popping a butterscotch into her mouth, she listened to the older woman talk about her ultrasounds.

"We had to drink about thirty-two ounces of water to have a full bladder. They told me it was to make the uterus float so the picture would be better. I was floating all right. I floated all over myself on the way to the appointment. I was smart enough to bring a towel in the car for the next one. Try explaining that odor to everyone. I told them stray cats got into my car." Cass laughed as Lauren's face turned bright red at the memory. "Are you sure you don't want anyone to come with you? I have a lot of time available that needs to be used by the end of the year."

"No, no. I'll be fine. Dr. Basara says everything is looking good and this ultrasound will just confirm that the baby is developing normally."

Cass removed her sweater as she headed off the elevator into the parking structure. The August heat was hanging on with an attitude, she thought to herself. Who can breathe in this stuff? Getting in her car and turning the air on high, she giggled as she pictured Lauren wetting herself on the way to her appointment. Cass couldn't imagine sharing that sort of information with anyone, and was pleased that Lauren considered her friend enough to do so.

Cass regretted turning down Lauren's offer to accompany her to the ultrasound and pulled her cell phone out, trying her direct line. Her voicemail picked up the call directly. "Hey Lauren, it's Cass. I changed my mind. I guess I would appreciate your company. If you get this message, meet me at the ultrasound clinic at Mercy General. My appointment is scheduled for 1:20."

Disappointed that Lauren didn't answer, Cass hoped that she would get the message in time to join her. She eased her car into traffic, thinking about the accident that preceded the news of her pregnancy. Seems a lifetime ago. She much preferred arriving at the hospital in her own wheels.

She gazed at the massive building as she pulled into the multi-tiered parking structure, knowing that somewhere behind one of those windows lay Caroline. Lauren hadn't shared much about her, but Cass knew she was dealing with memories long buried. For whatever reason, the events in Cass's life acted like a jack hammer in Caroline's memory, cracking the foundation and leaving jagged scars and deep holes in the facade of control Caroline cultivated. Lauren visited with her a few times each week.

"On some level, she's sorry for what she's done to you, Cass. Please don't hold it against her. She needs her friends right now, and I think she would like to count you among them, if you would have her."

"*Really,*" Cass lingered on the word. She took a long minute to unwrap her lunch, glancing around the cafeteria.

"Think about it Cass. Your forgiveness would mean a lot to her."

"*Really,*" Cass said again, savoring the word. "I'm supposed to just pretend this never happened? Look the other way?"

"Cass, forgiveness doesn't mean that what she did to you was okay. I think most people misunderstand what true forgiveness is. Forgiveness doesn't excuse bad behavior or allow someone to get away with something, necessarily. What forgiveness does do is give the offended party, you in this case, room to walk away. It sounds funny, I realize, like it's backward or something, but when you choose to hold something against someone, you wind up hurting as much as they do."

Cass flashed hot and cold at this information. It was like Lauren was speaking directly into her soul, into an area that had nothing to do with Caroline.

"This is how I've explained it to my kids since I think they were born with score cards in their hands. Memories like elephants, never forgetting 'that one time'," she said by way of imitating her kids fighting with each other. "Forgiveness is a promise you give to someone that benefits yourself as well. You promise not to consciously bring to mind the offense, not to use it against the offender, and not to seek revenge for the offense."

At this, Cass's eyebrows shot up. "You mean I'm not supposed to make sure they are held responsible for something?"

"There is a difference between justice and revenge, Cass. Revenge often operates outside of the law and is seeking only to wound someone as they wounded you. Justice leaves room for the legal system, if necessary, to seek restitution on your behalf. Can you see the difference?"

"Yes. I never really thought about it like that. You've given me a lot to think about. I always thought that forgiveness meant giving someone a free pass, like being a doormat or something."

"Most people do. I did, before I met Mike. He helped me understand that much of my thinking was based on the world's perception, not God's. The Bible has a lot to say on the subject of forgiveness." A smile played at the corners of Lauren's mouth. "Have you opened that Bible you brought to the coffee night?"

"Not really, except to flip through it. I've read some of the small boxes of writing." Cass admitted. "Why?"

"Do me a favor. No, do yourself a favor. Look up Psalm 103:12. It's about forgiveness. It is the example that God sets for us to follow. Cass," Lauren said hesitantly, "I would love to talk further with you about this, if you would like. Not trying to be pushy or anything."

"Yeah, I think I'd like that too."

Promising to read the section Lauren directed, they set a date for a future conversation. Cass obligated herself to thinking about what had taken place with Caroline in this light, but knew that she had many opportunities to apply this new information.

Walking back to her desk from the lunchroom, Cass could feel her foundations beginning to shift. If someone asked her in the future when her heart began to change, this would have been the day she remembered.

Looking up at the five story hospital structure, Cass thought it strange that Caroline could be looking down at her from any one of those windows and she would never know it. Her mind flashed back to the events of the summer, culminating with the coffee night. Does remembering this mean I'm not forgiving her? What if I remember without getting angry? I can't help what comes into my head, can I? I'll have to talk to Lauren about this. East to west, she thought, recalling the scripture Lauren told her to look up. Cass wasn't really sure what this had to do with Caroline exactly.

Cass entered the labyrinth of the hospital, reading the signs that would direct her to the radiology wing where her ultrasound would take place. Stopping at the first restroom she saw, she giggled again at Lauren's disclosure. How embarrassing that must have been, showing up with wet pants for a doctor's appointment. Still chuckling, she opened the door and saw Lauren about ten feet in front of her.

"Hey there!" she called. "You did get my message!"

Lauren spun around at the familiar voice with a smile on her face. "Thanks for calling me! I'm happy to be here, and happy to be out of work early," she confessed.

"Just don't tell my mom. She'll be ticked that I didn't invite her. Seems like everything I say opens a can of worms with her. Remind me of this conversation when my own kids are complaining about me!"

"Kids? Are you planning more?"

"Who knows? It's not like I planned this one," she said, chagrined.

Lauren stopped walking for a minute and turned to face Cass. "You may not have planned this baby, Cass, but God did. God did."

Something about that statement brought tears to Cass's eyes. Crazy hormones, she thought, even though she knew there were more than hormones to her reaction. It was like every time Lauren said something about God, something new fluttered in the pit of Cass's stomach. She envied the woman's faith, her deep conviction in the rightness of God in the face of the wrongness of practically everything else.

They resumed their route to the ultrasound lab where Cass was given a clipboard and some papers to sort through. After a few moments, a young Asian man wearing green hospital issue scrubs and a badge identifying him as Abe Nguyen called her back, and she motioned for Lauren to follow.

The trio entered the brightly lit room; a window looked out over a courtyard lush with flowers this time of year. Cass wondered if the building was structured so every floor got a courtyard, appreciating the value of a place to go and decompress during the work day. As she admired the view, the attendant pulled the blinds closed. "Sorry. The screen is easier to see without the light coming through the window." He instructed her to hop on the table, and at that they all laughed.

"I haven't hopped anywhere in a while," Cass said.

"That's my best joke for expectant women," Abe smiled. "I love that one."

Just then the door opened and the radiologist entered the room. "Thank you Abraham." The young man nodded and left the room. Cass saw the tube of goo, a stack of paper towels, and the ultrasound wand on a stainless steel tray. Everything looked sterile, surgical almost.

"I'm Dr. Simmons. I'll be performing your ultrasound today."

Leo Simmons was in his fifties with close cropped gray hair and an easy smile. He reminded Cass of Marcus Welby, MD, a show she liked to watch as a child. Who was that actor that played him?

Shaking hands, she was ready to introduce him to Lauren when the woman greeted him first. "Leo, I didn't know this is where you worked. You think you know somebody . . ." her voice trailed off in a laugh.

"Cass, Leo, Dr. Simmons, is a deacon at our church. I've known him for years, but we won't hold that against him. I'm sure he's quite capable."

Cass appreciated the easy banter that filled the room; it eased the anxiety she didn't realize she was feeling until she felt herself sigh.

"I guess I *was* a little nervous."

"How do you know each other?" he asked, addressing the question to Cass.

"We work together, and Lauren offered to come with me to this appointment. My mom couldn't make it," she fibbed, knowing she hadn't wanted to ask her in the first place. She ignored Lauren's glance in her direction.

After washing his hands, Dr. Simmons sat on his stool near the ultrasound machine. "Shall we get started?" He motioned to Lauren to turn off the lights. "What have you decided about learning the sex of the baby? I don't promise that we will be able to make it out clearly, because sometimes they just don't cooperate, but we can try if you would like to know."

Cass shook her head, saying that she thought she would just keep the surprises coming.

Adjusting herself on the table, she tried not to think about the fact that her pants were unzipped to the point of showing her girl business. She flinched slightly as the goop hit her abdomen. Dr. Simmons laughed, saying that they try to heat it up, but the viscosity needed to convey the images is lost as the gel thins out. We settle for not freezing, he said.

Cass watched as murky images began to fill the screen. Small x's appeared where the doctor marked off various measurements.

She could see little toes in the image, and the pebble path outline of the baby's spine. A flood of emotion caught her by surprise, seeing her baby for the first time in person. Her awareness of him or her changed from the abstract defined by kicks, nausea, and heartburn, to a clearly revealed person living inside her. She was going to be a mother and here was her child; overwhelmed with longing to feel his little head snuggled under her chin, she imagined shiny black hair and little squinted eyes. She laughed as he waved his arm, waving back at the screen.

The wand froze for a moment as the doctor increased the magnification, staring at the monitor. Cass eyes darted from his face to the screen; she swallowed hard as she studied his eyebrows furrowed close together, trying not to grow alarmed.

She watched as he switched screens to one containing her personal information. He seemed to be looking for something in particular. With a sharp exhale, he switched back to the murky underwater scene.

"Cass, let me show you something." He zoomed the image out. "This is the sac containing your baby. From everything I have seen, he, or she," he said, catching himself, "is developing normally. Right here," he traced an area that she struggled to interpret, "is another sac. Did Dr. Basara say anything about twins, because I don't have that in my paperwork anywhere."

The room spun as Cass thought she heard the word twins. Certain she had misunderstood, she looked to Lauren for clarification. She was not reassured, however, to see the woman's mouth hanging open as far as hers was.

"What? What are you saying?" her voice a whisper. For news that would be good even if not entirely expected, the doctor did not seem excited. He seemed concerned.

"With the technology we have, we can confirm the due date by comparing the measurements of the baby's development. Most babies develop at the same rate, no matter what size the parents are. Certain markers, like organ development and brain size, are not impacted by how big a baby might weigh at birth." He paused, giving her a moment to absorb that information before going on.

"This larger sac confirms the EDC, the estimated date of confinement, as January 24th. This sac, while markedly less developed, confirms the same date, but there are issues here."

Cass bristled at the term issues, feeling protective towards this unexpected, but as Lauren had told her, not unplanned, child. "What can you tell me?" She struggled to keep her voice from wavering, the fear building just under the surface.

"Sometimes, when twins are developing, one of them takes the first share of the nutrition and oxygen, leaving the other twin to develop on less than sufficient resources. But that only happens with identical twins, not fraternal, as yours are. This means that each have their own placenta, their own food station, if you will. With this little one, I need to make some more measurements to ascertain what is happening here, if in fact I can."

He traced the tiny skull, leaving a trail of x's as he did on the bigger baby, confirming that the conception did occur at the same time. "The brain and the heart are developmentally on target, but something isn't squaring up."

Lauren took Cass's hand as the doctor continued his exam and gave it a squeeze. Tears leaked out of the corners of Cass's eyes as she lay on her back, trying not to panic at this news.

"The heart is tiny but strong, Cass. Have you ever heard of Vanishing Twin Syndrome?"

Cass shook her head as the doctor continued. "Sometimes in a pregnancy of twins, one of them has a fatal abnormality, something going on that doesn't allow them to develop normally. A chromosome doesn't trigger an event that needs to happen, and development ceases. The embryo is absorbed into the mother's body, often before she even knew she was having twins. It happens occasionally that on early ultrasounds with fertility patients, twins are seen at six weeks and only one embryo at ten weeks. Rare but not unheard of.

"I don't want to speculate God's plan here," he said, glancing at Lauren for permission, "but in my professional opinion, this may be the early stage of a later term Vanishing Twin Syndrome. But I never claim to understand what He may be up to," he finished solemnly. "I've seen enough things in my career that should have gone one way go the complete opposite."

"What is it? The baby, what sex is it?" Cass asked in a small voice.

"A girl. A tiny girl. I'm sure that Dr. Basara will want to monitor this pregnancy much closer from this point forward. I will be in touch with her this afternoon, and you should expect a call from her in the next few days."

Dr. Simmons entered a few more calculations; Cass heard the printer jump to life. A series of black and white photographs streamed out of the machine. The doctor walked over to retrieve the pictures, keeping one set for himself and handing one to Cass, enclosed in a folder that said "Baby's First Pictures."

"I will be praying for the best outcome, Cass. I know this is not what you expected today."

"I am hearing that a lot lately," Cass reflected wryly.

CHAPTER 21

Lauren waited quietly as Cass cleaned herself of the ultrasound gel and finished dressing. She could see the weariness on Cass's face as she picked up the folder containing the pictures of her babies.

"I feel like I'm planning a birthday celebration and a funeral at the same time. How can I be happy and heartbroken at the same time?" Cass's voice broke. "I don't know how many more roller coaster rides I can take."

Putting an arm around her shaking shoulders, Lauren told Cass of a chapel on the first floor in the hospital. "It's usually empty. I've stopped in there a few times when I've been to see Caroline. Would you like to stop there and talk for a bit before heading home?"

Cass allowed herself to be lead from the radiology wing to the first floor chapel without resistance. The room was understated; candles adorned a table in the front, wooden pews in two rows for seating, and a gold cross positioned in the center of the front wall. Bibles lay on the seat every few feet or so. The lighting was dim, as if the designer knew that this place would be sought for solace not celebration. Several groups of chairs upholstered in faded cabbage rose print completed the space.

"These chairs remind me of my grandma's house," said Cass, choosing one to sink into.

Lauren reached for one of the Bible's and opened it, handing it to Cass to read. Cass, shaking her head, asked Lauren to just read it to her. Softly, Lauren began to read aloud from Isaiah:

"But now, thus says the Lord, your Creator, O Jacob,
and he who formed you, O Israel,
'Do not fear, for I have redeemed you;
I have called you by name; you are Mine!
When you pass through the waters, I will be with you;
And through the rivers, they will not overflow you.
When you walk through the fire, you will not be
*   scorched,*
Nor will the flame burn you.
For I am the Lord your God,
The Holy One of Israel, your Savior."

Lost in thought, Cass noticed that Lauren had finished reading and looked up, tears shining in her eyes.

"He knows my name? God knows who I am? Is this where that radio station gets their logo from . . . He Knows Your Name?"

Lauren nodded, hope bursting in her heart but trying to keep her face neutral.

"Then why is He doing this to me?"

"Oh, Cass, God isn't doing anything to you. His ways are not our ways; it says that a little later in this book. What He does promise is that you aren't taking one step, one roller coaster ride," she said, giving Cass's phrase back to her, "that He isn't willing to take with you."

Lauren paused, waiting for that to sink in. "Nothing happens in this world, good, bad, or indifferent, that hasn't passed through God's filter. Nothing surprises Him or catches Him off guard. The difference comes in how we respond to things that come our way. We can choose to let life break us down, or we can choose to see things through God's eyes, knowing how He feels about us.

"Besides knowing every hair on your head, every breath you will take, He already knows your babies. May I read something else to you?" she asked, turning the pages of the pew Bible backward a few pages. "Psalm 139 reminds me that God doesn't make anything by accident."

She began to read again, her voice as dewy soft as the faded fabric on the chairs.

> *"For You formed my inward parts;*
> *You wove me in my mother's womb.*
> *I will give thanks to You, for I am fearfully and*
> *   wonderfully made;*
> *Wonderful are Your works,*
> *And my soul knows it very well."*

Lauren paused in her reading to hand Cass a tissue from her purse. The tears streamed freely down Cass's face, unable to contain herself any longer. Lauren knew Cass was at a crossroads and would have some things to sort out.

"What are you thinking, sweetie?"

"I know this is supposed to make me happy or something, but honestly, I feel like I'm losing my rights. I feel like, if I get okay with God, I lose my right to be upset about anything."

Lauren nodded thoughtfully, not condemning her answer. "May I finish this Psalm, Cass?"

"My frame was not hidden from You,
When I was made in secret,
And skillfully wrought in the depths of the earth;
Your eyes beheld my unformed substance;
And in Your book were all written
The days that were ordained for me,
When as yet there was not one of them."

"Cass, what do these words say to you?" Lauren asked softly, having learned in her counseling training to assume nothing.

With a gulp, Cass confessed these words made her angry. "Every day I'm going to live, and that my babies are going to live, God already knows what's going to happen? But He just stands there? What kind of garbage is that?

"I don't know what to think. If God is so good and knows so much, why does he let things like this happen? I think," she said slowly, "that these verses are supposed to make me happy, but honestly, they tick me off. He can see my babies, yet let my daughter be formed in a way that might kill her?" Her voice rose shrilly. "He could see all of my days but let my dad leave? I don't know how to make sense of this. I just don't. Right now I just want both of my babies to be born healthy. What is He doing about that, do you suppose?" She felt bad about sounding so sarcastic to Lauren, knowing that none of this was her fault, but was powerless to stop herself.

Cass watched as Lauren's expression never changed. She just let her carry on until she wore herself out.

"Cass, I don't claim to understand or have all the answers. I don't want to offer you the canned Christian answer. All I can do is tell you what I know firsthand." Taking a breath, she continued. "God has a plan for your life, and your babies' lives, no matter how many days, months, or years He gives them. He doesn't force us to do what He wants; He wants us to love Him and trust Him out of our own free will. When life hurts us, it isn't because God is mean. It is because He has given each of us the right to make our own choices, and sometimes people make choices that wound us. What He does promise is to be there with us the whole time. When your dad left your family, God was just as sad as you were." She paused, waiting for a reaction. Receiving none, she continued. "What we don't see today are the things He protected us from. We will never know this side of Heaven all the ways God worked in our lives. But believing that God is good is a choice. You could just easily decide that He is a vindictive angry god bent on making our lives miserable. You would find no shortage of evidence to back up your claim. Faith is a choice, Cass. It all depends which filter we use to screen our information." Lauren stopped, knowing she was on the edge of overloading Cass with information she wasn't capable of processing yet.

"I'm going to write down a few scriptures, a few verses, that you might find helpful as you look at today's events. You are not alone; God is here, Cass, even if you don't see Him, and I am here for you too, to answer questions, to yell at, or just to sit with you. No pressure, okay?"

"I feel like I'm in a basket at the top of a waterfall, with one branch that just might save me, if I can reach it. I'm just not sure if it can hold my weight." Cass nodded slowly as she spoke. "One thing I know . . . I'm glad you were here with me today."

147

CHAPTER 22

Cass stooped down gingerly to pick up the house keys she'd dropped, hands not cooperating with the bombshell that she was having not one but two babies. Seeing the fragile girl on the monitor required all the reserves of self-control Cass possessed. She knew she would not escape scott-free. Where did she get off thinking she would just go on and live happily ever after? Happily ever after doesn't happen to people like her. A price needed to be paid for the mistakes she'd made, right?

Swinging open the door to her light flooded apartment, she wandered down the hall that would be the baby's room. Correction: babies' room. Surveying the items she was beginning to collect here and there, turquoise and lime green blankets, yellow crib sheets, a high chair she saw at a garage sale she drove past, all those things waiting expectantly for a life to give them purpose.

Cass reflected that she was a mirror of those things, waiting expectantly for a life to give her purpose as well. She'd been living in a sort of limbo for the better part of her life, never sure of the reason for her existence. Never really somebody's wife, except for that short stint out of high school, not really feeling like someone's daughter, nobody's sister . . . maybe that's why

I've grabbed on to this pregnancy with both hands. I finally get to be somebody to someone. I get to be someone's mommy.

"Oh, God, if you can hear me, please let me be mommy to both these babies. Please God, don't take her. You can do this. You can do this one thing for me, God. Please," she begged.

Cass collapsed on the soft fleece baby blankets she'd bought, smelling the cottony freshness in them. She hugged them to herself, all the fear and tension of the past few hours melting away for the moment. She sat up, feeling the rustle of the paper Lauren had given her stuffed in the pocket of her maternity jeans. Unfolding it, she read Lauren's neat script:

> "Cass, these words bring me comfort. I pray they comfort
> you as well.
> Philippians Chapter 4 verses 6-8 (in the New Testament)
> Psalm 139-all of it (Psalms is almost in the middle of the
> Bible)
> Isaiah chapter 43 verses 1-4 (a few books after Psalms)
> Isaiah chapter 55 verses 1-8
> Jeremiah chapter 29 verses 11-13 (right after Isaiah)
> These are God's words to the people He loves. Please call
> me, anytime. Lauren"

Cass took a few deep breaths to compose herself. Okay, God. Okay. Let's check you out. She headed to her bedroom to retrieve the Bible she'd bought for the event at Lauren's church, the binding still relatively uncracked. As she sat down to look up the first one, that Philip place, she remembered her dad's backpack in the front closet.

Cass tiptoed down the hall like she might wake someone and went to the front hall closet, opening the door slowly.

Resting where she'd left it after reading the letter her dad had written to her, the pack seemed to consider her as well. She wiped her hands on her jeans, aware of an uncomfortable sweat that had nothing to do with the weather.

She reached for the handle and dragged it towards her, sitting right there in the entry way to go through it. Cass pulled out the carefully wrapped letters she'd replaced into their zip locked tombs and the grocery store paper wrapped book. Her father's Bible. Overwhelmed enough by the discovery of the pictures and letters, she hadn't the energy to go through the Bible.

With all the upheaval brought on by Caroline's breakdown, the knowledge that there was more to look through in the back pack simmered on her back burner, waiting for the right time. Today was the right time, she figured.

Dad's Bible and the note from Lauren in hand, Cass curled up in the corner of the couch. Stanley lay next to her, purring his gratitude for her presence. She lifted the book to her nose, smelling the scent of cigarette smoke and butterscotch candy; a stray wrapper that had found its way in to the pages fell to her lap. Opening the front cover, she carefully paged through the tissue thin sheets, stopping at the scrawl on the dedication page. Someone had presented the book to her father, Landry Alan Parker, on March 20th, 1998, Center City Rescue Mission inscribed below the date. Almost a decade ago.

Cass paged through the Bible, seeing little notes and underlined phrases as she went. Her dad had a Bible and he wrote in it? Both struck her as oddities, the fact that her dad had a Bible that he wrote in, and that you were allowed to write in a Bible. *I thought writing in a Bible was against the rules.*

Lauren's note said that Philippians was in the New Testament. Cass opened to the front of the Bible, remembering distantly that a table of contents listed all the names of the books in it. Some had odd, unpronounceable names, she noticed. Finding the page number for Philippians, she turned to it, then looked for the correct chapter.

As Cass turned the page highlighted words jumped out at her.

"Be anxious for nothing, but in everything with prayer and supplication with thanksgiving let your requests be made known to God. And the peace of God, which surpasses all comprehension, will guard your hearts and your minds in Christ Jesus. Finally brethren, whatever is true, whatever is honorable, whatever is right, whatever is pure, whatever is lovely, whatever is of good repute, if there is any excellence and if anything worthy of praise, dwell on these things." *How to live free*, her dad had scribbled in the margin.

Free from what? Cass considered that this must be how Lauren didn't worry when her son was ill. She'd shared with Cass how she'd prayed over his crib, a diagnosis hanging in the balance, and felt at peace knowing that whatever happened, God had it covered. "It didn't guarantee the happy ending we were praying for, but in the middle of it all, we had peace."

A stillness filled Cass as she realized that she and her dad had both come to the same place for answers.

Be anxious for nothing? Bible speak for *Don't worry, be happy*? Did God know what was going on with her? Did he realize that one of her babies could be dying in her womb at this very minute? *Tell me, great and powerful Oz, how am I supposed to deal with that?*

Whatever is true, honorable, right, pure, lovely, dwell on these things? Only look at the good stuff? What about the bad stuff? What do I do with that? Ignore it and hope it goes away? She noticed the letters PYM written in small letters next to that verse. If she didn't have her glasses on, she would've missed it. PYM?

Okay, Dad, Lauren, and God. I'm trying here. Good stuff . . . I have a roof over my head. I have a job, despite almost losing it. I have a few friends, sort of. I am going to . . . be a mom. Okay, not feeling anything different. This is like the gratitude exercises the self-help gurus are always touting, Cass thought. What's so different about this? She looked again at the passage, and the words of verse seven stood out to her. She read them as if for the first time:

And the peace of God, which transcends all understanding, will guard your hearts and your minds in Christ Jesus.

Cass got this picture in her head of fiery angels standing around her, protecting her from all unwanted influence. That's what makes this different. Trying to only look on the bright side puts the effort and the result on her, she realized. These verses say that if she does these things, brings her troubles to God, He will do the work of bringing the peace.

If Cass's ears were tuned to the cosmos, she would have heard a flurry of conversation in the heavenly realms. "She's getting it!" While she couldn't hear that, she felt something relax inside, like a guard of her own being let down. For someone who prided herself on not needing anyone, she momentarily saw that as a weakness, not a strength.

Not needing anyone leaves no room to need God.

Before turning to the next verse that Lauren had written down for her, she let the wafer thin pages lead the way, thumbing slowly through them, reading the phrases her dad had highlighted and the small notes along the way. She settled in a book called Matthew. She'd heard of him; he was one of Jesus' followers.

Cass noticed that some of the text was in red in a few of the books. She flipped to the opening of the Bible, reading that the red-line text were the words Jesus Himself had spoken. Well, this ought to be good, Cass thought. Go ahead, give it to me straight.

"Come to Me, all who are weary and burdened, and I will give you rest."

This was not the condemnation and judgment she'd expected. This sounded more like an invitation, a door opening instead of a door closing. Was it possible she'd misunderstood this God thing all her life?

The singing in the heavenly courts got louder.

She took a long sip of her hibiscus mint tea, a splurge she allowed herself to purchase every now and again, and considered how her life might change if she didn't insist on carrying everything herself. "Come to me, all who are weary and burdened, and I will give you rest."

She thought of her relationship with Cato and the ones before him in this light. She'd been bringing burdens of loneliness to them wanting help carrying them, and they'd handed them right back to her. Could Jesus be trusted to take them?

This was taking Cass to a place she didn't often journey, deep inside her soul. She'd been afraid of what she'd find if she looked too close, preferring instead to just live each day within the reality it brought. The looking glass was beginning to crack and she was afraid of falling in.

What was next? She looked at the slip and saw "Psalm 139-all of it" written down. She appreciated Lauren's attempt to point her in the right direction with a location reference. Cass located the book of Psalms and located 139 without too much trouble, and began to read.

Tears stung her eyes as she read, for the first time, how intimately she was known by God. All the times she felt anonymous, like nobody would care if she ever showed up for life again, welled up as her soul was cleansed for the first time. Her thoughts in the chapel, angry with God, flashed as she read the verse that said that before a word was on her tongue, He knew it. How many times had that gotten her into trouble? Again here, she found her father's hand: "Search me O God, and know my heart; Try me and know my anxious thoughts; and see if there be any hurtful way in me, and lead me in the way everlasting."

The hurtful way part had earned a highlight and an underline. Curious, Cass thought, that he would be worried about being hurtful. She wondered if that verse had helped him heal from turning his back on his family.

"You know me, God. I am getting this." Cass rubbed her belly as her babies stirred within. She tried to picture them, inward parts formed perfectly and wonderfully, even if perfect and wonderful meant that one of them might not survive.

She looked at the notes she'd made after reading in Philippians: Focus on the good, and God will bring peace. She worked hard to train her mind on this, especially in regard to a child not being formed correctly. This is not what perfect looks like. Perfect is two parents in the home with healthy kids, letting her childhood rear up again. Focus, Cass.

Stretching from her position on the couch disrupted Stanley and he yawned his complaint, hopping down to find a more hospitable place. Cass rose, carrying her mug to the kitchen, her mind mulling over everything she'd read. The late afternoon sun invited her to her patio, the one Stanley had first claimed as his residence.

Grateful afresh for the westward facing apartment, she gazed on the mixture of colors a late afternoon sky brought. No box of crayons could capture this, Cass thought to herself. Azure blue, fiery pinks, and just the smudges of charcoal around the distant edges, heralding the coming evening. She leaned back, one hand on her belly, and tilted her face to the waning sun.

"Come to me" played in her mind, the desire to take that step closer irresistible. "Church isn't for people like us, Cassie" her mother's voice popped in out of nowhere, uninvited and unwelcome. That's not what she was reading. As far as the description went, weary and heavy-laden, she fit that perfectly. She skimmed the rest of the verses around that one, looking for her disqualification, and couldn't find it.

"Come to me." She remembered the pictures she'd seen of Jesus when she was a child on the Bible bus. He had kind eyes, and always seemed to be reaching a hand towards someone. These words were telling her the same.

"Come to me." Body relaxed by the sun, Cass replayed the letter from her dad in her head, having memorized most of it. He told her to find Jesus, and here was the Man himself extending an invitation to come.

Feeling slightly foolish as she stood and looked around, fearing someone might see her, she took one step forward. "Jesus, I don't know what you mean exactly, but I am coming to You. Okay?" Standing there, Cass did not know what to expect, a clap of thunder, a giant wind, a voice in the air. She stood for another moment, listening, unable to hear the cheering in heaven as the angels celebrated her arrival. Hearing nothing, and not feeling any different, Cass sat back down, feeling a little duped.

She resolved to work up the nerve to talk to Lauren about this. Surely she would know.

The shadows deepened as Cass picked up her dad's Bible, pulling out the bookmark of Lauren's note. Reading the first two parts had left her head swimming, but she was ready to start fresh.

Isaiah. That was a name she could pronounce at least. Everyone seemed to be naming their kids Isaiah. Now she knew where they got it. Turning to the chapter Lauren indicated, 43, she read the words, recognizing them as the ones she'd read earlier that day in the chapel.

"You know my name?" spoke into the air, pausing for an answer. Her chin dipped lower as she remembered the shame of being called by the wrong name by Cato. Not realizing how little she'd meant to him, being called "Mel" seared the rejection with as much force as a branding iron. "But You know my name," she said again, aloud. "I wish I could hear it."

Just then the phone rang, interrupting her one sided conversation with God. "Hello?"

"Cass, it's Lauren. Just calling to check in."

"Funny, I was just asking God to say my name." At the confused silence, she continued. "I am reading in the verses you gave me, and in this one, it says that God has called me by name. I was just thinking it would be nice to hear it spoken out loud, and here you are. Not quite the same, but it will have to do," she finished with a laugh.

"That's funny, Cass. That will be a great day indeed. But I don't want to keep you if you're busy."

"Lauren, actually, since you called, do you have a minute?" Cass screwed up her courage to ask her friend about coming to Jesus. She told of her taking the step on her patio but not feeling any different.

Lauren laughed warmly. "Cass, that's awesome. You know, it's different for everyone. Just like you read in Psalm 139, God knows your thoughts and what's going on inside of you, even when we tried to hide it He knows. He's better and worse than a mom with eyes in the back of her head.

"You were right to interpret that as an invitation, and I'm so excited that you found that passage on your own."

"Actually, my dad found it for me." Confused silence ensued once again, and Cass shared that she'd been looking up the passages in her father's Bible, the one that had been in his backpack. "He had this verse underlined, and it caught my eye when I was thumbing through. The red colored writing and the yellow highlighting made it pretty difficult to miss."

"That is so amazin', Cass," emotion thickening her accent. "Do you want to read together? I can get my Bible."

"No, that's okay. I'm good."

Cass hung up the phone, feeling like she did when she turned down the offer of company for her ultrasound appointment. Why did she keep shutting the door like that? Picking up the phone, she scrolled to the last incoming number. Lauren picked up on the first ring.

"I changed my mind. I'm on Isaiah 55, and I don't get it."

"Okay, the meat of it starts in verse six, but I wanted you to read the part inviting you to come to Him, in verse one. His invitation does not require anything other than a willingness and a thirst. This is a little deep, but the Clif notes version is that Isaiah was a prophet who told people what God wanted them to know. Eventually, all the writings of the prophets, the Psalms of King David and others, and the early history of mankind came together to form the Old Testament. The New Testament is after Jesus was born. But, stop me before I can't stop myself. That is a lesson for another day. Suffice it to say that Isaiah was God's mouthpiece.

See that second set of verses, starting with verse six?"

"Uh huh."

"This is the part where God promises compassion to those who return to Him. People back then were used to a system of vindication and retribution . . . you've heard of an eye for an eye? Well, this speaks to the fact that God will handle our failures differently, that His ways are not our ways and His thoughts are not our thoughts. Especially in today's world with karma and what goes around comes around being the dominating thought, we don't understand grace any better than the Israelites did back then. But God's promise is that when we come to Him, He welcomes us. Everything in the Bible is meant to point to that promise."

"Who pays then? I've done things wrong, I know that. And what about other people? Who pays for the stuff they've done?" Cass didn't have to say it, but her thoughts of her parents, Cato, and most recently, Caroline, hung heavily in the air.

Lauren paused, and Cass knew she was giving her time to think it through for herself.

"This goes back to the forgiveness thing, doesn't it? God forgives me and I am supposed to forgive others. I looked up that other verse you gave me, well, actually I googled it," she confessed with a giggle, "and it said from the east to the west, or something like that. I'm supposed to hold what others have done to me the same way, aren't I. I still don't get who pays for it though. I feel like all the bad we do, and get, is just hanging out there in the universe some place, waiting to bite me in the butt," she said, mindful of her audience. Something about Lauren made her careful of her language.

"That is where Jesus comes in. You are right, if it weren't for Him, we would all be dragging a big bag of mess around with us. God does require payment for our sins, but because He knew we could never work them off, He allowed Jesus to pay the price. We'll sit down together and take a little trip down the Roman Road, as we call it, but basically, we celebrate Jesus paying the price we couldn't on the cross, and beating the punishment, which is death, by rising Easter morning. He is the only one who could do it, Cass.

"The only way we get to spend eternity in Heaven is through our relationship with Jesus. Not by being good enough, not by performing certain tasks or rites of passage, not any other way than accepting what He did for us on the cross. It's that simple, which makes it so hard to understand. Even I want to make it harder. I get caught up in trying to be the perfect pastor's wife, but that's a trap. No one is perfect, and God doesn't love me better when I act like it," the woman chuckled. "Feel free to remind me of that."

"Again, you've given me a lot to think about. And to think that I used to call you 'Vanilla Pudding Lauren'," Cass confessed. "You just seemed too nice to be real. Not that you aren't nice," she stammered, suddenly on unsure ground. "But you're real and nice. Dig that hole deeper, Cass."

Lauren rescued her with a laugh. "Vanilla Pudding Lauren? You just had no idea what lurked under the surface." Lauren's laughter reaped its intended effect, keeping Cass at ease. Lauren didn't offend easily and knew instinctively that anything Cass might have thought about her was birthed in a lonely place, not a malicious one. "How about you call me VP for short? It feeds that ego you didn't know I had?"

"Listen, VP, I've kept you long enough. These babies are hungry, and truthfully, my thoughts are swimming. I might go grab a pen and paper and see what flows. His ways are definitely not my ways, and I've got to figure out how to bring the two together."

"With Jesus, Cass. Good night, friend."

CHAPTER 23

Caroline rushed around her condominium, cleaning what was already spotless. New cleaning supplies lived under the kitchen sink, her latest obsession since committing to her doctor she would not pick up a razor. Instead, scrubbing became a new therapy. She checked her reflection, questioned her choice of clothing, and wondered for the millionth time what had possessed her to seek out Lauren.

She'd been a good work friend, and a faithful visitor to the hospital, but this was a next step, one that Caroline knew, on a visceral level, would change things. Forever, possibly.

She glanced out the window and saw Lauren retreating down the sidewalk, back to her silver SUV. Her silvery blonde hair lifting in the breeze, Lauren leaned in the driver's side window for a second time; Caroline could practically feel the exhale of breath as Lauren marched up the sidewalk. *Maybe she's as uncomfortable as I am . . .*

Running a shaking hand through her spiky jet black hair, Caroline responded to the buzzer. "Lauren. Come on up."

Opening the door, Caroline was aware once again how even though she was a good four inches taller than Lauren in bare feet, the petite woman possessed an air of confidence that didn't come from her stature. Dwarfed by her presence, she offered Lauren the comfortable chair and perched on the edge of her gray leather sofa. It maintained its store bought stiffness despite being three years old. Her living room had yet to be lived in.

"Caroline, you look well. Time off agrees with you."

"A trip off the deep end does a body good, apparently," Caroline agreed with a subdued laugh. "I am ready to get back to work though. Too much time to think does not do a body good."

Lauren's raised eyebrow spoke the question her lips didn't.

"Don't worry. I haven't been cutting. Look," she said, rolling up the sleeves of her silky turquoise t-shirt. "Clean."

This has the feeling of a first date, Caroline thought. Awkward pauses where easy banter usually lived, uncertainty charging the air.

"Caroline, I wasn't—"

"No, Lauren. It's okay. It is right of you to wonder. I'm trying to handle things differently than I used to. Cutting was a release for me but I didn't know what was driving the need. Does that make sense? I mean, how do you not know what you are thinking about?"

"The mind is a wonderful creation, made by a wonderful Creator." Caroline shifted sharply in her seat.

"If He is so wonderful, why did He let my father do what he did to me? If He is so wonderful, why didn't my mom stop Him? Even when I told her. Why didn't she stop Him? If He's so flipping wonderful, why didn't He protect me?"

The tears on Lauren's cheeks stopped Caroline short.

"I'm so sorry, Lauren. I just have so many questions. You know, where was God in all of this? I went to church. I made my communion. I did everything I was supposed to, but He let me get hurt." Caroline spoke from a distant place, needing to ask questions that had no answer. "God left me."

"No, Caroline, He didn't. He never did. For whatever reason, and I can't speak for God, but for whatever reason, He allows things in this life that hurt. But from those broken places flows new life. His Word promises it, Caroline. Maybe you have heard the saying 'Believing is free but faith costs a lot'? Faith costs, Caroline. Sometimes more than we are willing to pay." Reaching for the tissue Caroline offered, Lauren took a deep breath and continued.

"I asked many of those same questions when I was fifteen. Growing up as PK's, preacher's kids, my sisters and I were raised pretty strictly. The whole church was watching, you know," she said with a smirk. "We made it our mission to break as many of those rules as we could. When I was a freshman in high school, a boy invited me to a party my parents would never have allowed me to attend." Drawing a shaky breath, she went on. "So I went without their permission. Turns out there were no parents home, as this boy had promised there would be. Someone's older brother had dropped off a case of beer. I didn't want to look nerdy, so I took one when this boy offered it. One thing led to another . . . slow dancing, kissing, an offer to take the party somewhere more private. Before I had a chance to recognize what was happening, this boy was on top of me. I tried to fight back, but, well . . . I couldn't. I can't say he stole my virginity, but I sure didn't give it up willingly."

"Oh, Lauren, I'm so sorry."

"Turns out he collected ten dollars from each of his buddies who bet him he couldn't get a PK like me into bed. I lost my virginity for a fifty dollar bet. I was too ashamed to tell my parents, but I didn't need to. When the rest of the school found out, my parents heard through the small town grapevine. They were horrified, both for me and for their reputation in the town. In the middle of one discussion," Lauren making the quotations sign with her hands, "my mother asked how I could have done that to them. Like I set out to ruin their lives or something. I felt dirty and ugly. And once you feel dirty and ugly, unless someone tells you you're not, you approach life differently. I earned my own reputation for being promiscuous. I knew I'd already disappointed God by disobeying my parents, so I kept moving farther away from Him."

"What changed for you? You obviously aren't far from Him now."

"He sent Mike for me, and Mike told me that God had already sent Jesus for me."

"Didn't you know that already? I mean, being a preacher's kid and all?"

"Not in a way that mattered. I could recite tons of Bible verses and knew all the songs—Jesus loves me this I know—but not in a way that mattered to me personally. You know John 3:16?"

"For God so loved the world—?"

"I thought of it as the world in general. Not as in me, Lauren Crosby, in particular. Jesus came for all the sins I had committed and would commit. He came to make me clean in God's eyes. Because God loves us so much, He sent His Son to pay a price we couldn't. Even if I hadn't snuck out that night, I still wouldn't be good enough for God without Jesus."

Caroline chewed on her lip, Lauren's words hanging in the air between them. "I don't think you get my question. If God is so good, so good that He sent His son for me, why didn't He stop my dad from hurting me?"

Lauren leaned forward and took Caroline's freezing hands in her own. "Caroline, I don't have an answer for that specifically. But, what I have learned is that God is sovereign. He is bigger than anything that could ever touch us. He can take the worst, most unimaginable situations, and breathe new life into them. He can take all the hurts we carry away. He can clean us and heal us of all the garbage that this world throws at us. None of us will get out of here unscathed, untouched, because this is not heaven. Not to go all deep churchy on you, but this world is the devil's playground. Jesus defeated him through His death on the cross, and in the last days, he will be bound for all eternity. But in the meantime, he's here, making a mess of things.

"What God *does* do is promise to never leave us to face him on our own. He promises to strengthen us to handle anything that comes our way. He promises to give a purpose to our pain. Nothing can exist that is bigger than God's ability and desire to deal with it. And, maybe He allows certain things into our lives to shape us into the people He desires us to be. Not that He wants to see us hurt, but, again, He can redeem any situation. He can take the muck and turn it into something that glorifies Him, something that draws others to Him. That is His purpose for each one of us, you know. To be His witnesses and help others come closer to Him. This is where faith costs something.

"Caroline, look at me."

Caroline's head hung low, the tissues in her hand now shredded confetti.

"I can't do this. I can't let this be okay for any reason, not even for God."

"Caroline, don't misunderstand me. God is not saying that what happened to you, or to me, is okay. What He says is to trust Him with it. Let Him turn your life into something beautiful. Let Him bring healing to the places of rage and fear. What happened to you should never happen to anyone, along with a thousand other things that should never happen to anyone, but God allows them. Faith says that God doesn't allow anything into our lives that He can't use for His purpose. Can you give it to Him? Can you take what your dad did to you, and what your mom did to you, and give it to God?"

Caroline jerked her eyes from Lauren's and closed them against her intensity.

"Are you going to let the enemy have this victory in your life? Because he wants it, Caroline. He wants it. Every time you choose to hang on to the past, Satan rejoices. He doesn't want God to be enough. Don't give it to him." Beads of perspiration shone delicately on Lauren's forehead. The emotion, palpable. "Let God in. Let God in and start healing the past."

Caroline's face, still pale beneath her Mediterranean coloring, wore bright red spots, her complexion mottled with anguish. Never had she felt such a tug. Hating, hiding . . . these came naturally to her. Giving something up, giving up a right to something . . . this was not how she did things. Caroline knew that Lauren was not the only one waiting for an answer. She could feel unseen eyes waiting for her decision. She had never heard it put such a way. Let God have it, or give the victory and control over to the enemy. *He doesn't deserve your forgiveness*, the enemy hissed in her ear. *Without this to hang on to, you will be empty again. First they took your razors, now they want to take this.*

But overall, a knowledge that did not come from her own mind flooded her. She knew Lauren had shared truth with her. God could do something different with her life. He could take the pain, but He wouldn't pry it out of her hands. She had to offer it to Him.

Caroline leaned back hard against the couch cushions, hands falling open at her side. "I can't keep going like this. I need something . . . I need God. This is just too heavy, Lauren. I can't do this anymore."

The tears came, but instead of bitter, ugly tears, she cried tears of freedom, of finally letting go. Caroline could feel Lauren take the seat next to her on the couch. As the older woman circled her shoulders with her arm, Caroline stiffened briefly, but then leaned in close, savoring the warmth of another person for the first time in many years.

The late September sun flooded the room with golden brilliance. Caroline looked up and met Lauren's eyes.

"I think God is smiling on my decision."

"I think you're right."

Caroline reached over and turned off the alarm clock, despite the fact she'd been up for an hour already. Her leave of absence officially over, she showered for her first day of work since her breakdown.

A banana at the counter covered breakfast and with a last glance in the mirror, she fought the butterflies, grabbed her briefcase, and headed to the parking garage. *This feels like the first day at a new school.*

DEBBIE GIESE

Pulling into the parking lot, she was surprised to find that the building looked exactly the same. She was the one who was different. *Would everyone see that? I wonder what stories are going around. Truth is definitely stranger than fiction, that's for sure.*

"Ms. McKay, pleasure to see you."

"Thanks, Roberto. Good to be back."

Caroline let out her breath as the elevator doors opened to her floor, unaware that she'd been holding it in the first place. Cass's eyes were the first she met exiting the elevator. *And so it begins . . .*

"Hey, Caroline. We are walking to the coffee shop for lunch if it doesn't rain. You in?"

"Um . . . yeah. Yes. Thank you for asking."

The questioning glances of her co-workers held no judgment or pity, something else she hadn't wanted to face. Heading to her office, she officially began the new chapter in her life.

Reaching for her phone she dialed the number she'd tried a million times to forget.

"Hi, Mom. It's Caroline. Is dad there?"

CHAPTER 24

Cass checked and rechecked her grocery list. Thirty five years old and just learning to cook a turkey. What was that all about?

"How is it you never learned to cook a turkey? I mean, weren't you married before?" Cass had learned not to take offense at Shelby's directness.

"Big meat intimidates me." That got a round of laughs from the table. "I'm serious. Ham, turkey . . . ostrich, I'm afraid I'll screw it up. Chalk it up to fear of failure," Cass said with a smile. It felt good to laugh at herself in the company of friends.

"Cass, don't forget to take the bag out of the turkey," Shelby teased in her good natured way.

"My first turkey was like that one in the Chevy Chase movie. Turkey jerky by the time I was done," Lauren added."I don't know where I got the idea it needed to cook all day, but that's what I did. Cooked that bird all day, took it out of the oven to set while I finished the vegetables and all the skin jumped back off the bones. I screamed out loud, thinking it was going to start flying all around the kitchen," she finished, laughing at the memory. "We had a houseful from the church and they all ate it anyway, poor things. Probably stopped at McDonald's on the way home for some real home cooking."

"My mashed potatoes were gray." Everyone looked at Caroline, surprised at her contribution to the conversation. "I still don't know why," she said, shaking her head.

The lunch table was alive with conversation, memories of birds past, and friendship. For the first time in recent memory she anticipated the upcoming holiday with pleasure.

Cass had called Geri, suggesting that they do something different for the holiday.

"Mom, what would you think about having a real Thanksgiving this year?" Cass proposed, her voice ringing with excitement.

"What do you mean a *real* Thanksgiving? What do you think we've been doing?"

"Mom," she began carefully, caught off guard by Geri's abruptness, "meeting in the middle at Denny's just doesn't feel right to me this year. And besides," she coached," I'm going to be a mother. I need to learn how to cook a turkey. I think it's a requirement," she said, hoping to lighten the mood.

That's the trouble with mothers, she thought. Touchy, touchy, touchy. She hoped she wouldn't end up like that.

"So, what do you think? Want to help me learn to cook a real Thanksgiving dinner?"

"Well, if you're sure that's what you want. It's a lot of work, Cass. A lot of time on your feet . . . chopping, stuffing, stirring, are you sure you're up to all that?"

"I feel great. I've got my energy back, and I'll move the stool into the kitchen if I need to sit. Tell you what; we can still get a pie from Bakers Square. Then we don't have to worry about dessert. Deal?"

"Deal," her mother said slowly. "Now Cassandra, grab a pen and paper. We're going to have to make a list." Cass heaved a sigh of relief as she began to take notes. Round one. Done.

The preparations underway, Cass checked her cart against the list to make sure she had everything her mother told her they'd need.

Big frozen turkey. Check.

Russet potatoes. Not the red ones, Cassandra. Russets. Check.

Three packets of turkey gravy, McCormick's brand. Don't cheap out on the store brand, ok?

Celery, onions, poultry seasoning, stuffing cubes, sausage . . . what is the sausage for? I don't remember sausage at Thanksgiving. Links or patties?

Stealing a glance in the carts of other shoppers, she saw sausage in the meat case packaging. Ok, meat case sausage it would be. Check.

She added a small can of sweet potatoes and a few cans of green beans and corn, just to make sure she had a selection. Her mother promised to pick up dinner rolls.

Cass headed to the beverage department to pick up some sparkling cider for a festive touch. Maneuvering the cart and her belly through the crowded aisles was proving tricky even though she was shopping on a Friday night. Backing up to try and reach her destination another way, she felt someone clip her ankles with their cart.

Not sure how anyone can miss me, Cass thought to herself sarcastically. She turned to see who the errant driver was and found herself staring into the steely eyes of Caroline; truthfully, Caroline appeared as mortified by the whole thing as Cass was.

If Cass was learning anything from Lauren, it was how to take the high road.

"Hey Caroline. Come here often?"

"Not usually."

Cass glanced in Caroline's cart, spying a few Lean Cuisine's, one of which was a turkey dinner, an expensive bottle of Riesling, and a frozen pie.

"Cooking this year?" Cass asked, hoping the question didn't sound like she was prying.

"No. I decided not to travel home. Going light," she said, gesturing toward her cart. "On the upside, no dishes to wash."

Scarcely aware she was talking, Cass heard herself invite Caroline to join her and her mother. "I can't promise much except company," she finished lamely, hoping at the same time for acceptance and rejection of her invitation.

"I'll think about it." Caroline spoke as though showing up would be doing Cass a favor.

The stakes felt much higher as Cass finished up her shopping.

The office closed early Wednesday after the company provided a holiday lunch. Heading to her car, Cass was surprised to find Caroline leaning against it.

"What time tomorrow?"

"Huh?"

"For dinner. I'll bring dessert."

"Um . . . oh, how about 2:00?" Cass fumbled, going for nonchalant but not able to pull it off.

"Fine."

It was one of those *fines* that didn't feel all that fine.

CHAPTER 25

Cass vacuumed her living room carpet for the second time before bed, vowing to give it a quick once over in the morning. *How do you end up in these situations, Cassandra? Your mother and Caroline. Seriously.*

Leaning sideways over the bathtub since her belly prohibited her from reaching it straight on, she scrubbed the porcelain finish, wondering if anyone would peek behind the shower curtain anyway. Not taking any chances, she stepped in to the tub to shine the stainless fixtures.

Cass found herself flat on her back, shower curtain draped across her midsection, the smell of disinfectant filling her nostrils.

"What the—?" Too stunned to cry, she took stock of her situation. She threw the shower curtain onto the floor, gripping the edge of the tub with her right hand to pull herself into a sitting position.

Okay. Okay. I'm alright, she breathed, reaching up to feel a lump forming on the back of her head. Last time I clean the tub for anyone.

Wincing, Cass reached up for the hand support and pulled herself to a crouch, exhaling slowly as the pounding in her head increased. No concussion is going to stop this Thanksgiving dinner. With a deep groan of exertion, Cass forced her way to her feet, and, holding the wall for support, gingerly stepped over the edge of the tub onto dry ground.

The hand mirror confirmed a small goose egg. At least my hair covers that, she thought wryly, considering how much worse a broken nose or black eye would look and feel. Her motivation going down the drain with the cleanser, Cass fixed herself a cup of tea after checking the turkey's progress one last time. Still frozen, but not as frozen as yesterday. "Thaw, baby. Thaw," she coaxed.

Cass woke the next morning earlier than usual after a fitful night of sleep. Between the dancing babies and the throbbing knob on her head, sleep hadn't come easily. In the midst of the tossing and turning she had nightmares of serving hotdogs for Thanksgiving dinner.

With gravel filled eyes, Cass went to check the turkey, dismayed to find it still relatively solid. She pulled out her computer and googled frozen turkey. Following the website's advice, she undressed him from his plastic garments and stood him up in the sink to run water through him. He looked a little macabre, balancing on his two legs as she held him by the headless neck. This turkey weighs twice what the babies will weigh, she realized. At least I know they'll fit in the sink.

Grimacing, she reached in to find that bag everyone and their brother had told her to remove. Cass was beginning to wonder why people just didn't make a nice steak for Thanksgiving. She filled the sink with cold water and left him to bathe while she dressed for the day.

Taking some pain relievers, Cass chose a pretty cream colored dress for the occasion, one that matched her new apron. She was taking this holiday hostess role seriously. Slipping into her dress, she took a moment to study herself in the mirror. Except for the black suitcases under her eyes, she looked pretty good. The baby caused an increase in the amount of blood being circulated, her doctor said, giving her that glow the rest of the world is trying to figure out how to bottle. Satisfied with her appearance, she permitted herself a few minutes of the Macy's Day Parade as she waited for her mother's arrival.

Cass prayed that the day would bring celebrations and new beginnings. "Dear God, please help me to start fresh with everyone. Help me to move forward. I need it, this baby needs it, my mother needs it, and heck, Caroline probably needs it too. Amen."

Taking a deep breath, Cass rose to respond to the buzzer that announced her mother's arrival. Genuine smile firmly in place, Cass opened the door.

"Now Cassandra, I hope you don't mind, but I brought a friend. Mack, this is my daughter, Cassandra. Cassie, Mack." Awkwardly, the duo shook hands, as Cass took in Mack. Six foot two and eyes of blue, as the song sort of went, filled her doorway, gray pony tail gathered neatly at his neck, flowers in hand.

"Cassandra, pleasure to meet you," he said, offering the flowers as an apology of sorts. "I told your mother I would stay home and see her later, but she insisted."

"Please, come in. Come in," she said more firmly, moving to open the door wider. "You are very welcome, but I make no promises. This is my first turkey," she laughed, wondering when she had gotten so chatty.

Mack's eyes crinkled as he met hers. "I can probably do a little something about that."

"Mack's a chef, Cassie."

"Not really, but your mother insists on calling me that. I know my way around the kitchen, though. A bit of a hobby of mine."

Cass led them to her kitchen where the turkey was resting comfortably in the sink filled with cold water.

"I got that bag out, rinsed the ice chunks out, and let him finishing thawing. He was still a little frozen this morning.

Mack's sharp eye took in the kitchen, noticing the under the counter radio sitting on top of the counter.

"I could mount that for you once the bird is in the oven, if you like," he offered.

"Actually, I . . . well . . . ok. I don't know what I was waiting for, actually," she admitted. "I guess I just didn't expect to be living here this long, but it's been three years already. I should probably finish moving in."

"No need to explain. I'm happy to do it for you," said Mack kindly. "Now, let's see about this bird."

Rolling up his sleeves, he washed his hands at the sink, narrowly avoiding filling the bird bath with soapy water. While he was getting the turkey settled and dried off, Cass showed her mother the room that would belong to the babies.

"I've started getting a few things. I figure I won't need two cribs set up right away. They will sleep in bassinettes for the first little while, and can probably share a crib for a few months. I picked out this bedding, mom. What do you think?" Cass removed a huge department store bag from the closet revealing a nursery set in soft buttery yellows and mossy greens. "I figure this will look good for both of them. Do you like it?" Glancing at the woman she'd known all her life but felt like she was still getting to know, Cass found herself suddenly very concerned about her mother's opinion.

"It's lovely Cass." Something in her tone did not reflect the graciousness of her words.

"What?"

"*What* what?" her mother replied innocently.

Cass searched her mother's face, noticing the furrow settling between her eye brows. "You sound like you don't really like it."

"I don't know, Cassie. I feel like you are trying not to need me, to keep me separate from all this. I guess I'm feeling left out. We never really got to plan a wedding, and now I don't get to help plan for the babies. I guess I just feel like you don't need my help with anything."

Cass rolled her eyes inside her head, where her mother wouldn't see. Seriously. The woman didn't want to be a mom when she needed one, and now that she was about to be a mother herself, her mom suddenly wants back on the scene? Remembering that just this morning she prayed for new beginnings, she took a deep breath.

"I wasn't trying to make you feel left out. We don't live close by each other, and I am doing the best I can to get ready for them on my own, because I am on my own." Cass smiled at her mom. "Is there something special you would like to do, or something you would like to help with?" Cass rubbed her back to relieve the tightness beginning to set in. That was one thing she and her mother had in common: they both carried their stress in their backs.

"Well, I could crochet a blanket for each of them, green for him and yellow for her. Then they would match the bedding. It's nice, by the way." Geri reached for Cass's hand. "And maybe, if you like, I can stay for a few days after the babies are born. You *are* going to need a hand. What would you think about that?"

"Sure, mom, that would be great. It will probably be harder than I even realize."

"Ladies, if I could invite you to the kitchen . . ." Mack called down the hallway.

"You are going to have to tell me about him, mother," seeing how Geri's face lit up at his voice.

"Later. You'd never believe it anyway," she said with a mischievous smile.

"Cass, let me show you a trick I learned. You will never have dry turkey again."

Mack laid the turkey breast side up on a clean kitchen towel. He grasped the bird by the neck, and slid his long fingers under the skin, loosening it from the breast meat to create a pocket. Cass was amazed by the amount of room in there as Mack stretched the skin out.

He'd been busy while they were chatting in the nursery mixing a few tablespoons of butter with some different spices he'd garnered from Cass's cupboard. He even sliced an orange into thin coasters, and grated some of the orange peel. He took the butter mixture and patted a layer between the skin and the breast of the turkey. He took the orange slices, a cut up onion, and some celery and placed those into the smaller cavity of the bird.

"We'll save the big cavity for the stuffing. Cass, can you start sautéing the sausage? You did tell her to get sausage, right? Geri, you start dicing the onions and celery."

The two women stood there, mouths hanging open, both unaccustomed to having a man in the kitchen telling them what to do. Cass was unaccustomed to having a man in the kitchen, period. This was new territory for her altogether.

"You didn't tell me you were bringing Gordon Ramsey with you," she chuckled in the direction of her mother.

"Gordon Ramsey!" Mack said in mock horror. "Try to do a girl a favor," he muttered, drying his hands on the towel. "I shall go where all shunned men go, to find a parking spot in front of the television."

Both women did as he'd directed however, he noticed with a smug grin in their direction.

"Small dice, Geri. Small dice," he said, dodging the towel she flicked at his backside.

Cass took a closer look at her mother, traces of the prettiest girl in the whole eighth grade still there. Her skin had aged a bit due to the rays of the sun she insisted on living under from June through September. "Cassandra, I don't drink, smoke, or eat too badly. If I don't lie in the sun I just might live forever. Me and Keith Richards," she'd joke.

With chestnut hair, courtesy of L'Oreal to be sure but still thick and wavy, the smattering of freckles, the wide-set hazel eyes, even teeth, and small dimples in her cheeks, Geri was still cute by anyone's standards, but at her age perky was becoming the adjective of choice. She hated that. What was she supposed to do? Stop living?

Cass noticed that her mother seemed extra lively in the presence of Mack and found it sweet. She knew her mother was lonely and hadn't had an easy life, often settling for companionship over character. If the past thirty minutes were any indication, Mack seemed to have the whole package. She could hear the drone of the television and took the opportunity to question her mother about him again.

"So mother, what is the mysterious meeting story?"

"I hit him."

"What?"

"I hit him in the parking lot of the complex where we live. Never met him before that, but if I had to plow into someone, he was a pretty good choice," she laughed.

"You never told me you had an accident!"

"It was hardly anything, just a fender bender. We exchanged information, had a few conversations, then a coffee together, then . . ."

"Mother! I don't want to hear anymore!" Cass feigned shock. Truthfully, nothing would shock her, but she was genuinely happy for her mother. Mack seemed like a good guy. And he cooked!

"How's it coming in there, girls?"

"Fine," they hollered in unison, giggling. This felt good to Cass, side by side with her mother, talking and cooking. Just being mother and daughter. Geri scraped her cutting board of chopped veggies into the drained pan of sausage and let that work together. Taking over the cooking lesson, she directed Cass to add some thyme and poultry seasoning to the pot and let everything cook, stirring occasionally.

Grabbing the bag of bread cubes off the counter, she stirred these into the mix.

"Was there always sausage in stuffing?" Cass asked. "I never noticed."

"There are a million stuffing recipes, Cass, but the good ones always have sausage. Your father," she stopped to examine Cass's response, "your father liked this wild rice dressing, but I never did get a taste for that. Just didn't seem natural, but I guess it depends where you grew up and where your people are from."

"One man's normal is another man's weird, that's for sure."

Cass reached for a butterscotch candy from the little dish on the counter, stiffening as she overextended her arm. She could feel the muscles right up the middle of her back as they rebelled against the stretch.

"You okay?" Geri inquired.

"Yeah. Just a little tight today," she said, rubbing her belly. "No big deal."

The stuffing mixed, they decided not to invite Mack back into the kitchen, enjoying the easy conversation. Geri instructed Cass to pack the cavity with stuffing lightly.

"We can put the extra in a casserole to cook."

Mack came in the kitchen, feigning indignation at not being consulted.

With the turkey in the oven, there were potatoes to be peeled but not much else to do right now. Cass mentioned to her mother that she'd invited someone from work to join them.

"Oh?" Geri asked, eyebrows rising.

"A woman, mother. Just a woman named Caroline. She wasn't making the drive home this year. Seriously mother, have you looked at me? I'm not exactly reeling 'em in these days." Cass gestured toward her midsection.

"I have looked, and you are beautiful."

"Just like your mother," Mack agreed. Geri blushed in pleasure.

"Cass, do you have a drill? We can get that radio mounted now."

"What would I have a drill for?" she asked with a grin. "Would an electric screwdriver suffice?"

"It'll have to. Note to self: bring own power tools to Cassandra's house."

Within fifteen minutes, Mack had the little stereo mounted under Cass's cupboard. He turned it on to check out his handiwork.

"All of creation, sing with me now. Lift up your voice and lay your burden down. All of creation, sing with me now. Fill up the heavens, let his glory resound." The music of Mercy Me filled the kitchen.

Geri looked quizzically at Cass. "What are you listening to?" she asked, checking the dial. "The religious station?"

"The Christian station. Not the religious station, mom. There's a difference." Feeling suddenly annoyed, Cass wished she didn't have to explain herself to her mother

"Mom, this station makes me happy. I can't explain it. And sometimes, when I read in my Bible," laughing at the expression on her mom's face, "I find the same words that

I sing along with. It's like singing the Bible. The same way I learned conjunctions . . . Conjunction Function," she sang.

"The Bible isn't for reading by regular people, Cassandra. You have to be a priest or something, a minister, to understand it."

"Actually mom, that's what I always thought, too, but it's not true. Parts of it *are* difficult to understand, at least for me still, but parts of, well, they just make me feel good. I can't explain it. What I can tell you is that I finally figured out that God is for me. Even when it feels like no one else is. He knows my name, mama."

Geri contemplated her daughter's revelation, wondering what else had changed. She did seem a little gentler, if that was the right word. Less tightly wound than normal.

"What else you got?" Mack asked, electric screwdriver revving in his hand.

"What about the football games?"

"I'll catch the highlights later."

"Well, since you asked, follow me." Cass lead him down the hall to the spare room, the nursery, she corrected herself. "Feel like putting some baby things together?"

"I thought you would never ask."

Mack got busy assembling the bassinet first, then tackled the crib.

"You are a lifesaver, Mack. I wasn't sure how I was going to get this all put together."

"My pleasure, Miz Cass. My pleasure," he drawled.

Geri got the bedding package out and removed the sheets, asking Cass what other baby laundry she had. "Might as well get it all set up, right?"

The savory smells of dinner cooking and the way the nursery was coming together tugged on Cass's emotions. Her eyes filled as she surveyed her surroundings. "Sorry. Hormones must be a little whacked today," she said, wiping her eyes. "My back, too. I'm going to put my feet up for a bit. Mack, I'll holler the play by play while you keep working."

Cass didn't notice Geri's eyebrows come together in concern as she watched her make her way down the hall.

CHAPTER 26

The doorbell rang just as Cass was inhaling the aroma of tradition. "We should have done this a long time ago," she thought to herself. Taking a deep breath, she opened the door, vowing not to be nervous at the thought of spending a whole afternoon with Caroline, unguarded.

If Cass had looked at the window, she would've seen Caroline's car in the lot an hour ago. Nerves played through as she wondered at the absurdity of spending a holiday with the woman she'd tried to get fired. Since that day Cass came to see her in the hospital, she seemed genuinely committed to letting bygones be bygones.

Two weeks into her hospital stay, Caroline had heard a light tap on her door. Her eyes widened as she recognized Cass in the doorway.

"Lauren suggested I stop by. She said you would be okay with it, even though I told her she's crazy." Red-faced at using the crazy word, she back pedaled. "I mean, out of her mind."

"You have a gift for digging holes, Cass." Caroline observed wryly. "It's okay. Have a seat. I was a little crazy. Maybe still am, who knows. The jury's still out."

Cass watched a hornet crawling on the outside of the window, not sure that she was on the safer side of the glass. She sat on the offered chair, taking in the room. The bed was typical hospital issue, but the bedding and the clothes Caroline wore were obviously her own. Even though Caroline had savagely cut off her own hair, somehow Lauren's friend was able to style it into an adorable pixie cut.

"Short hair becomes you," she offered lamely. Cass swallowed, the discomfort creating a lemon in her throat. What was Lauren thinking?

"Listen Cass, I told Lauren to invite you." The hollowness was still evident in her cheeks, but some of the hunted look she'd carried in her eyes that night at the church had faded. Whatever she was dealing with, she was turning the corner. "I'm dealing with a lot of muck, a lifetime of mess really, and don't have a lot to offer anyone right now. But I asked Lauren to invite you because I owe you an apology."

Cass didn't know how to respond. In the face of Caroline's mental health issues, she felt like she should downplay the past few months. "Oh, no, Caroline, that's okay. I'm fine. Really. You were under a lot of stress."

"I'm the one who tipped Rollinger off." Caroline let that settle for a minute.

"What? How?"

"For whatever reason, you were a catalyst for me. One of them anyway. You may or may not know this—I know how Shelby runs her mouth on—but I used to be married. My husband left me for a woman he worked with on April 23rd, 2004. On top of everything else, I hadn't fully dealt with that yet, or the reason he left." At that, her voice trembled and she reached for her bottle of water, taking a long drink as she regained her poise. Cass had never seen her as anything but composed and controlled, until that night at the church.

"Seeing you and Cato together—you weren't fooling anyone, you know. Anyway, seeing you together stirred up a lot of emotions." Caroline met her gaze squarely and continued.

"That day he was ending things, apparently, I followed you. Remember I jumped up and left at the same time you did? I parked in the motel lot and took pictures of you entering the room, and then the two of you leaving. I emailed them to Rollinger. You were my target, but Cato got fired." She continued, her affect flat, like she just needed to get the details out. "I couldn't stand to see you getting away with everything, sleeping with another woman's man. I wanted to blame women like you for breaking up my own marriage, even if that isn't entirely accurate, I'm realizing."

Cass continued to meet her gaze, waiting for her to finish. Reliving the embarrassment of being called into a conference with Mr. Rollinger and knowing Caroline was behind it all . . . that was going to take some processing. And Cass wasn't sure she'd actually heard an apology, although she was well aware of the other woman's pain running under her words. She could tell that Caroline was still on shaky ground, despite the efforts she was making towards her own recovery. As Cass waited to see if Caroline offered anything else, she could hear Lauren's voice in her head. "Forgiving someone does not require an apology on their part first."

Not quite believing her own ears, Cass heard herself say, "Caroline, I forgive you."

"Why?"

Taken aback by the question, Cass answered, "Because if I don't, I will be the one to suffer. Forgiveness is given, not earned." Lauren would be so proud, she thought.

"You've been talking to Lauren!" Caroline smiled genuinely for the first time. "She's been telling me the same thing."

Standing in the doorway of Cass's apartment, Caroline considered that this was a step in the right direction. She needed to build good connections, at least her therapist said so, and she could sense in Cass a kindred spirit. Each of us is running from something; we might as well jog it out together.

"Are you going to invite me in?"

"Uh, of course. I'm sorry, just in a little daze for a second. Come in."

"It smells wonderful in here. I thought this was your first turkey," Caroline said, handing Cass a white box tied with a string. "Pumpkin cake roll, think *jelly roll* but a million times worse for you. Not that it matters for you right now," she said with a glance towards Cass's belly. "How is it going? Being pregnant?"

"Feel right here," she said, laying Caroline's hand on her abdomen. "This is where the punter lives. And over here," she said, moving her hand down to the side of her abdomen, "is where the future tap dancer is working out."

"Is she . . . ?" Caroline had heard the talk about one of Cass's babies not growing well.

"The longer she stays in, the better. It's too bad the punter," as she'd taken to calling him, "can't come out on time and let her simmer for a bit longer."

With a grimace, Cass reached for the counter. She took a breath and at Caroline's alarmed expression said, "Braxton-

Hicks contractions, just practice ones. But if this is pretend, I can't imagine what the real thing will be like." Exhaling, she invited Caroline down the hall to meet her mom and Mack. "She brought a guy. Without asking, but whatever. He seems nice and he *is* putting together all the baby gear for me."

Introductions made, they did as women of countless generations have done on the Thanksgiving. Potatoes, peeled and chopped were set to boil, sweet potatoes opened and dumped into a saucepan, and rolls put on a tray to be browned once the turkey came out. Cass directed Caroline to the plates and silverware, grateful for the woman's willingness to help out even though she was there as a guest. I guess we're all family on a holiday, she thought with a smile. Maybe there is a friendship here.

The pain knifed through Cass's midsection at the same time she heard Caroline scream, "Cass! The blood!"

CHAPTER 27

Blood raced down Cass's legs as she struggled to understand what was happening. She looked to see if Caroline had lost it completely and stabbed her, feeling ashamed as she did so. Fear set in as she realized Caroline was still at the table, a stack of dishes in her hand. Geri looked on in horror, knowing exactly what was happening. She'd seen it too many times. Cass was losing her babies.

"Get some towels!" Geri hollered at Caroline. What was wrong with that girl? It's like she was frozen.

"Mack! Cass is in trouble! Get some towels!" Mack was halfway down the hall at the sound of Caroline's first scream, but did as he was told. He might know his way around the kitchen, but this was a little out of his comfort zone.

"Caroline! Girl, snap out of it! Call an ambulance!" Geri continued to bark orders.

"What's the address here?" Caroline asked in a panic stricken voice. Despite her recovery, the sight of blood brought out strong reactions. Mack thrust a piece of mail in her hand, and she read the address to the 911 operator. "Hurry. Oh please, please hurry." She began to sob quietly. "I never meant for anything bad to happen."

Following the instructions of the operator, they helped Cass to lie down and elevate her legs. The sirens announced the arrival of help, and Mack ran out to meet the ambulance driver. "I don't know what happened. One minute she was fine, the next, she's gushing blood."

The rescue technicians wheeled the gurney down the hall and into Cass's apartment, bringing calm to the situation. The man at the forefront took in the scene, glancing at Caroline for a moment too long. She looked away hastily.

"Ma'am, can you hear me?" The color drained from Cass's face as shock set in.

"Ma'am, Cass, stay with us." Quickly, they loaded her up onto the gurney, strapping her securely for safety, and wheeled her to the waiting ambulance. Mack volunteered to stay behind and hold down the fort as Geri trotted behind the men taking care of her daughter.

Caroline stood rooted to the spot, unsure of her place, ultimately opting to follow in her own vehicle. Calling Lauren, she filled her in on the little she knew. The town passed by in a blur as Caroline kept pace with the ambulance.

Inside the vehicle, the first responder tried to sort out the information. Geri gave him the name of Cass's obstetrician, telling him that her daughter was expecting twins. "I should've known what was happening," Geri lamented. "She'd been rubbing her back all morning, but I just figured she'd overdone things."

The ambulance wailed its way into the bay and Cass was quickly unloaded and sent up to the maternity ward. The fluids administered in the ambulance were working to revive Cass and she was able to answer a few questions as the doctors worked quickly to discern what they were dealing with.

"Have you had any trauma recently? Falls or anything like that?"

Cass confessed to slipping while cleaning the shower head the night before, but didn't want to alarm anyone. Except for the lump on her head and the ensuing headache, she felt alright. "My back hurts all the time anyway, so I didn't pay any mind to that."

Performing an ultrasound, the doctor turned to Cass. "Cass, what you are experiencing is called a placental abruption. Think of the placenta as the interface between you and your child. When you fell, it triggered the placenta to begin separating from the wall of the uterus. The ultrasound shows us that it is a moderate separation, not fully disengaged at this point. We are going to monitor you and your fetus here in the hospital and determine a course of action. Of course if the contractions continue, we will have to deliver the baby."

"Which baby is it?" Cass asked, fearing the worst.

"Well, if there is a silver lining in this, it's the fact that it is the larger of the two. And he is positioned so that a vaginal delivery is possible, as long as an emergency situation doesn't develop. I need to consult with Dr. Basara, of course, but I think we have a little time to monitor things here before making any decisions." With that, he left the room after giving instructions to the labor and delivery nurse working triage.

Cass glanced over at her mother, a worried frown creasing her face. "Mama, it's not your fault. You had no way of knowing I'd fallen. I wanted the whole house to sparkle," she said, intending a laugh but finishing with a sob. "Mama, I'm so scared."

"I know, baby. But you are stronger than I was, and these babies are bigger already than mine were. Things are going to turn out fine, you wait."

Cass listened to her mother's words with the reassuring swish of her babies' heartbeats playing a perfect counterpoint to one another. As long as she could hear that, Cass knew her babies were hanging in there. She stared at the twin monitors, trying to understand the different readouts, but knowing the one with the jagged line instinctively. The tightening of her uterus continued, the vise-like grip on her midsection evidenced by the spike of the graph on the paper feeding out of the machine. She knew a team was paying attention on various computers throughout the floor, but would have felt better to have a nurse by her side.

As if on cue, a tap on the door announced not just the nurse but Lauren and Caroline. "I came as soon as Caroline called. Oh my goodness, Cass, what do you have going on here?"

"Housekeeping almost did me in." Glancing sheepishly at Caroline, she confessed to cleaning the shower head in case anyone peeked behind the shower curtain.

Lauren chuckled about the dangers of housework, smiling at Cass's mother. "I'm Lauren," the woman said, extending her hand. "You must be Lauren's mother. You favor each other."

Cass and Geri looked at each other and laughed. "I never saw it until recently, but I guess we do," Cass said.

"Geri Parker. Pleasure. Wish we were meeting under better circumstances, but Happy Thanksgiving."

"I need to use the bathroom, please," Cass told the nurse, looking around the room at the immediate concern on everyone's face except Caroline's. Using the official term,

Cass announced that she needed to have a bowel movement, NOW. The nurse moved to close the curtain as Lauren ushered Caroline out of the room. The nurse explained to Cass that what she was feeling was the baby's head pushing down, creating the need to push similar to a bowel movement. Let me do a quick exam," she said, directing Cass to bring her heels together and let her legs fall apart. The exam confirmed her suspicion that the labor was progressing rapidly and she called the doctor on duty just as Dr. Basara was entering the room.

"Doctor, it looks like we are having a baby."

With lightning speed borne of professional training, a team of nurses came in with a heated isolette. The bed was quickly disassembled to become a delivery table, and Cass was prepared for delivery. Due to the size of the baby, the team knew that it wouldn't take much pushing before he made his entrance, and because he was not full term, complications were possible.

In the hallway, Lauren and Caroline could see by the flurry of activity that delivery was imminent. "Father," Lauren prayed, "only You know what is going to happen here today. Lord, please, please, be close to Cass right now. Watch over her babies, keep them safe. I thank you in advance for all You are going to do. In Jesus Name, Amen." Lauren raised her head, then quickly lowered it as Caroline picked up the prayer.

"God, I haven't been the best to Cass. Please help her today. Don't take her babies, God. Please don't take her babies." Wiping the corners of her eyes, she saw Lauren smiling at her. "What?" she asked with a grin. "She needs as many prayers as she can get right now."

"My thought exactly." Lauren took out her phone and called Shelby first, then the prayer leader for the church, filling in the details for Mike.

The room swam as Cass screwed her eyes shut and pushed for all she was worth. How can one tiny baby cause so much pain? Trying to focus on the nurse's voice, Cass tucked her chin down, grabbed her knees, and gave a mighty heave, feeling the white hot pressure as her baby's head shot from her body. Quickly instructed to cease pushing, Cass tried to follow the direction. Dr. Basara suctioned out the baby's mouth and Cass was given the go ahead to finish delivering her son.

Almost eight weeks early, he still managed to announce his presence with a lusty howl, as if protesting his early arrival. After being held up for Cass's approval, he was whisked to an exam table in the room for a more thorough inspection. Weighing in at five pounds ten ounces, and seventeen inches long, he sported the jet black hair of his father.

Cass felt the pressure of the placenta completing the delivery and held her breath. Dr. Basara had told her that if the contractions stopped on their own, there was a possibility of her daughter remaining in utero.

"It sounds impossible, Cass, I realize, but it's called delayed-interval delivery. In cases like yours, when only one twin is at risk of an early delivery, it's possible for labor to cease on its own and allow the second twin time to develop to a more viable size. Especially in your case, this is the outcome we are hoping for."

The room was silent except for the wails of Cass's son objecting to his first bath. All eyes were on the monitor still showing the state of Cass's contractions. With the delivery of the placenta, the waves were receding until just a few twinges remained. While the heartbeat of the second twin had shown some distress during her brother's delivery, it had recovered to a normal range.

"Cass, you may just have more to be thankful for this year than you even realize. This may be the chance your daughter needs," Dr. Basara said, astonished. "I have never seen this personally, only read about it. While the nurses take care of you, I'm going to consult with some fellow physicians on your case. Congratulations, mama. The boy looks beautiful."

Cass nodded to her mother, and told her to meet her grandson. "A boy, Cassie, we have a boy." The pain of losing three sons still echoed, but Geri knew that with the birth of this grandson, a new generation of promise was born.

After providing a soothing bath, albeit delivered bedside, the nurse helped Cass put on a fresh gown. She confided that this was the most unusual delivery she'd ever witnessed. Normally when one is born, they both just come out. "You must have a special guardian angel watching over you." Cass just smiled.

With Cass presentable, Geri invited Lauren and Caroline to meet her grandson. The pair entered the room with Shelby right behind them. "I couldn't stay away. I mean, my goodness, Cass, pumpkin pie can wait."

Despite his prematurity, Cass's son was breathing on his own well enough to spend a few minutes with her. He would be monitored closely in the neonatal intensive care unit, but Cass was permitted to hold him briefly. For all his ethnic coloring, he looked like a papoose swaddled tightly in his blankets. Cass gazed at his face, wondering at the life she and Cato had created, a brief twinge of guilt that she hadn't told him he was going to be a father.

She put the tiny bundle to her nose and inhaled deeply, the indescribable freshness that clings to newborn skin. Like the smell of heaven, Cass thought. She looked from her son to her mother, then to the faces of her three friends, speaking softly so as not to disturb the infant.

"Ladies,"

"And gentleman," interrupted Mack who had slipped in unnoticed. "Couldn't miss the day my best girl becomes a grandma, could I?" he said, squeezing Geri.

"And gentleman," Cass continued with a soft laugh, "May I present my son, Jason Landry Parker."

The oohs and aahs were silenced by the sharp intake of her mother's breath. "Mom, there's something I need to share with you, but not today, okay?" she pleaded with her eyes. "Today is full enough."

"That's an understatement," chortled Mack, missing the significance of the child's name.

A nurse from the NICU came to bring the tiny infant to the specialized nursery where he would be monitored closely. Events in the life of a premature baby move at a much faster pace with much higher stakes than for full term babies. Cass hugged her son, inhaling that other-worldly smell one more time, reluctantly releasing him into the care of the nurse.

Dr. Basara re-entered the room to discuss the care plan for Cass and her unborn daughter. Lauren, Caroline, and Shelby took the opportunity to bid their friend a final congratulations, heading home to share the miraculous events with their families, Caroline choosing to join Lauren and Mike for an evening service at their church, a Thanksgiving tradition.

"I'm sorry you missed dinner, Caroline," Cass deadpanned.

Tears shining bright, Caroline responded, "You've given me so much more, Cass. So much more."

As her guests left, Dr. Basara laid out the plan. "To begin with, Cass, we will perform a cervical cerclage, which is basically a suturing of your cervix to keep it from dilating. Antibiotics will be administered to prevent any infection to either you or the child. We will keep you in the hospital as long as your son is in the NICU, as bed rest will be necessary until you deliver. When your son, Jason, right? When Jason is ready to go home, we will discharge both of you, on one condition. Someone needs to be there with you at all times. Your activity level will be limited as a precaution. Is there someone available to provide care for you and the baby until you are delivered of the remaining child?"

A long moment passed until Cass felt her mother's hand on her arm. "Cassie, would you let me help you?" Cass turned slowly towards her mother, hesitating until the words from Lauren's conversation on forgiveness came into her head. "It's time, Cass. You've made peace with your dad. Give the same gift to your mother while she's here to receive it. She needs it as much as you do."

Cass nodded slowly at her mother, then looked at Dr. Basara. "My mother can stay with me."

CHAPTER 28

One week until Christmas. Cass felt she got the best gift already. Normally the holidays emphasized the emptiness that had plagued Cass most of her life. Cass knew the emptiness came from within, not from anything anyone had done. "Don't make other people responsible for your buttons, Cass." Another *Laurenism*, as she and Caroline had taken to calling Lauren's words of wisdom.

Caroline had been a fixture in Cass's room during her hospital stay, bringing magazines and treats not authorized by the doctors. She'd even painted Cass's toe nails when she'd complained of feeling like a beluga. Not even a baby one, she'd lamented.

Baby Jason was bundled into a royal blue Christmas stocking the day of his discharge; he was three weeks old to the day. Jason's twin sister was thriving, putting on the weight that, for some unknown reason, she was unable to do sharing a uterus. Everyone joked that she was already a diva, demanding her own room. "Good luck with that one, Cass!" her friends teased.

Sitting next to Cass one day in the hospital, Geri put down her crochet hook and the project she was working on. "Why are you so mad at me?"

The question caught her off guard, but she knew it was time to clear the air. "Mom, back in August, two police officers came to my work. They were carrying a back pack that belonged to daddy." She paused as the blood drained from her mother's face.

"Lan?"

"Yes, mama," Cass nodded, reverting to the childhood name, confirming the unasked question. "Mama, the back pack was found in a car, along with his body. My name was in it, Sandy Parker, and it took them close to six months to track me down. Mama, he'd written me a letter, saying that he should have fought harder to stay."

Pausing again, she gave her mother a chance to absorb what she was saying. "Mama, you told me he left us. His letter made it sound like you made him leave."

The question hung in the air.

"Oh, Cassie. Your father and I had problems I barely understood. I don't know how to explain them to you. We were each other's best medicine and worst poison. With each miscarriage, the distance between us grew as we blamed each other. Eventually we were only poison to one another, and then somehow, you were born. We tried to make it work, but you can't go backwards. We couldn't find the way. We just couldn't find our way."

Her voice broke, a combination of shame and relief flooding through her. "I made mistakes; we both did," she added quickly. "I asked him to leave, Cassie. I'm so sorry. I thought I could do better. I'm so sorry . . ." she cried, laying her head on Cass's lap.

Looking out her window, Cass weighed the words her mother shared against the heartbreak and regret in her father's letter. The truth lay somewhere in the middle, she was certain of that. Love and justice are not terms to be confused. Another Laurenism.

Cass's hand hovered over her mother's back, as if seeking permission from its owner to bestow comfort. Tears stung her eyes as she thought about her father, living and dying alone, somewhat by choice but mostly by circumstance. If she forgave her mother, did she dishonor her father?

Slowly, she lowered her hand to rest on her mother's shaking back. "It's okay, mama. It's okay. I forgive you. It's okay," Cass repeated, softly, until her mother calmed down, their roles temporarily reversed.

New beginnings in a season traditionally reserved for endings.

Geri and Mack arrived at the hospital promptly at 11:30, planning to head home after lunch was served. "I do not want to goof this up, Mack. You understand, right, honey, why I have to do this? Hurry up . . . are you sure we are going to be on time?" Geri about drove him nuts with her nervousness, but he smiled patiently. They'd had quite a few conversations since that day three weeks ago. He was planning one more, but figured that could wait until the second twin was born.

With choruses of Good Luck and the good natured ribbing of "See you soon" ringing in the air behind them, Cass and her son were loaded into Mack's SUV for the short drive home. It seemed a lifetime ago that she'd made the trip here by ambulance. She checked and rechecked to make sure Jason, Baby Jase as she called him, was still breathing. Cass had laughed when her mom told her she'd held a compact mirror to Cass's mouth checking it for fog; now she wished she had one on her. Feeling her daughter roll inside her and seeing her son face to face, Cass thought she would burst.

"Who am I, Lord, to deserve all this?" she prayed in gratitude.

Arriving home, Mack helped Cass out of the car while Geri carried the infant seat; he unlocked the door to Cass's apartment, swinging it wide. The soft glow of a Christmas tree lit the room, every branch laden with ornaments. Gifts of red and green, and pink and blue gaily wrapped lay beneath it.

"What? Who? How?" Cass looked around in wide-eyed confusion.

"Surprise!" came the whispered welcome. The lights came on to reveal Lauren, Caroline, Shelby, and a few other women Cass recognized from the church. Even Pastor Mike was there.

Lauren came for forward, arms outstretched to embrace her in a hug. "You missed Thanksgiving. We figured we'd celebrate Christmas twice as long."

Cass took in the scene, her throat thick with tears. She whispered again, "Who am I, Lord, that You should bless me like this."

"You guys," she said a little louder, "I don't deserve you. How can I ever thank you for everything? You even kept Stanley happy and out of the tree."

"Yeah, about that. He's out of the tree but I don't know if he's happy. We locked him in your room," Shelby clarified.

"Cassandra, what wonderful friends you have!" her mother sniffed, wiping away a tear.

The next week passed in a blur as the women settled into as much routine as life with a newborn affords. Mack made frequent trips, staying over on Christmas Eve. Cass opened the gifts in red and green Christmas morning, although she'd opened the blue gifts upon arriving home and was saving the pink ones for Jada's arrival, the name she'd chosen for her daughter. She couldn't keep calling her "the baby."

Gazing at the marvel of her son's face that Christmas morning, she contemplated Mary gazing on the face of her son. The fullness of motherhood upon her, she traced his cheek with her pinky, imagining Mary doing the same. How her heart must have broken, knowing who her son was but yet willing to give him life for us all. A completeness that was absent all her previous Christmases filled Cass as she pondered the greatest gift of all.

Christmas Day was a laid back affair. She'd begged her friends to stay with their families, except for Caroline. She wasn't ready to go home, and Cass welcomed her company.

On Christmas night, sitting with Geri, her son in her arms, Cass looked over at her mother. "You probably were the prettiest girl in the whole eighth grade, mama."

Geri watched as she reached into the pocket of her deep turquoise robe. That color becomes her, she thought to herself. Motherhood becomes her. Geri realized that Cass was holding an envelope out to her.

"What's this? You already gave me a card."

"This isn't from me, mama."

Geri reached for glasses and sucked in her breath as she recognized the handwriting. In script she hadn't seen in over twenty five years was her name. Hands shaking, she opened the flap of the envelope, glancing nervously at her daughter.

"Dear Geri,

It's been a long time. You were my childhood and my growing up, my life and sometimes my death. Geri, I'm sorry I wasn't the husband you'd hoped for. We both said a lot of things, but the only one I want you to remember when you think of me is this: I forgive you.

Find Jesus, Geri. He's not who you think He is.

I still remember you as the prettiest girl in the whole eighth grade.

Lan"

Geri handed the letter to Cass, the paper fluttering with the shaking of her hand. Reading the letter, Cass looked at her mother.

"He's right, mama. He's right."

CHAPTER 29

Cass woke the morning of January 16th, knowing somehow that this was the day she would meet her daughter. Calling Dr. Basara, then Caroline, she left her son in the care of his Mimi, as Geri insisted her grandma name be. "I mean, Cass, grandma sounds so old. I'm not that old, am I?"

"It's your fantasy, mom; make it a good one," Cass had teased her. "Mimi . . ." she'd said, shaking her head.

The intensive care she'd received allowed her daughter time to grow and mature, giving her the best chance possible of survival. Cass hugged her mother and laid eyes on her son, telling him to be good; she was going to be back with his sister before he knew it.

Her arrival at the hospital ignited a buzz among the staff. Never had twins been delivered seven and a half weeks apart at their facility. A few hours, occasionally, but even that was rare. Cass was brought to the too-familiar room. She listened with increasing anticipation as the swish-swish of her daughter's heartbeat filled the room, looking at Caroline with a grin.

"You sure you want to be my 'person'?"

"I'm all in, girl. I got this. I read everything you gave me." Caroline knew the real reason for the question and was grateful to her friend for checking.

Dr. Basara personally monitored the progress of her labor, watching as the peaks climbed higher and the valleys grew shorter. When the urge to push came to Cass this time, she recognized it for what it was, an invitation to meet her daughter. As the nurses staged the room for delivery, Cass focused on the regular swishing sound coming through the speakers, her eyes closed against all other distraction.

She heard it before the nurses. A few missed rhythms, the swishing growing sporadic. Cass heard one of the nurses speak Dr. Basara's name in alarm.

"Cass, we need you to push this baby out. Right now, Cass."

Chin tucked tight to her chest, Cass curled her whole body around her daughter's one last time, the force she exerted popping blood vessels in her cheeks. Someone would comment later that it looked like her laugh lines had been traced with a red pencil.

Cass grunted with the exertion of expelling her daughter, stopping at the command to wait one moment. She felt tugging and shifting, hands reaching inside as the doctor manually removed her daughter, one inch at a time.

There was no displaying the child for maternal approval. Cass kept her eyes pinched shut against the activity in the room. This was a nightmare she didn't want replaying every second for the rest of her life, knowing it would happen anyway.

One small cough emanated from the corner of the room, a team frantically trying to clear her airway and get breathing started. Cass would spend her nights running from that sound.

Seconds passed, then minutes. She felt Caroline's hand in her own, felt the nurses delivering her placenta and bathing her with warm water, just like last time. Only this time, no angry protests coming from her baby. This baby said nothing past that one cough.

"It's 5:12."

Dr. Basara's voice broke into her cocoon of silence. "Cass, I'm so sorry. The umbilical cord tangled around her neck during the birth process. She was just so tiny, Cass. She didn't have the strength to hold on. I'm so sorry."

The labor and delivery nurse approached Cass. Laying a hand on her shoulder, she softly asked if she'd like to hold her.

Cass wished she could stay underwater where she didn't have to deal with this, because then it wouldn't be real, right? Right?

"Cass, honey." Caroline's voice broke through. "Cass, I know where you are. You can't stay. Come back, Cass."

Cass slowly followed the voice to the surface and took a great gulp. She opened her eyes, blinded by the overhead light in the room. The nurse held a tiny doll swaddled in pink, rosebud lips sealed in a pout. Reaching for this black haired beauty, this impossibly small Polynesian princess, Cass waited to see those lips pucker and suck, rooting for a nipple, anxious to nurse this one; she hadn't been allowed to nurse Jase.

The lips didn't search. No sound filled the room outside of Caroline's sobs. Mother and daughter, locked in silence together, yet forever separate. Cass turned to look at Caroline and whispered, "Mary knows how this feels."

After a time, knowing that a minute is too soon and forever is not enough, the nurse came for the baby. She'd taken Cass through some paperwork, identifying her name for the records.

"Jada. Jada Dawson, for her Mimi."

Caroline had called Lauren, asking her to make the rest of the calls. Pastor Mike himself stayed with Jase so Geri and Mack could come say goodbye to Jada.

"I'm so sorry, baby. I'm so sorry."

Cass nodded stoically. "I know you know, mama."

Seeing Lauren for the first time, Cass looked at her and said, "It's not two birthday parties."

"Oh, Cass. He will see you through this."

CHAPTER 30

The spring winds were beginning to blow in off the plain, bringing with them the promise of warmer days. Just the promise, though, as today the air still bit. Bundled against the cold, Cass wondered again why the social worker wouldn't continue the conversation over the phone. She packed her son into his car seat and carried him to the car. Swaddling cover tucked firmly against the wind, she clicked him safely into the base in her backseat. As always, she double checked the safety belts, adjusted the mirror so she could keep an eye on him, and got into the driver's seat.

She checked her directions one more time as she headed for Patton, Ohio, a two hour drive in decent weather. Cass prayed for a safe drive and that the spring snowstorm hold off until tomorrow as the weatherman promised. Turning the radio to a soothing volume, she sang along . . .

Your love, O Lord, reaches to the Heavens . . . who knew that Holy Roller music could be so cool? Third Day, her new favorite group, filled the car with their song of hope.

Your righteousness is like a mighty mountain . . . your justice Lord, like the ocean's tides.

I will lift my voice to worship you my King.

And Cass did just that, singing praise to the God who had brought her such peace. Peace that she hadn't known or understood even six months ago. It was amazing to her that God would use the things He could have held against her to draw her closer. Glancing into the backseat, she knew that without the affair with Cato, she wouldn't have her son or the women she claimed as friends today. Jada's death left a hole, but it only glowed red hot some days now, not every second of every day. She didn't know how she'd survive if she didn't have Jase.

Cass drove the 115 miles thinking back to the day she had decided to go through her dad's backpack again. Since the baby's birth at Thanksgiving, she hadn't given it much thought, consumed and exhausted with new motherhood. She had spied it in the back of the closet when she was looking for her warm coat, and for some reason, it beckoned her closer. She opened the front pocket again, and as the business cards came into view, she wondered if the social worker listed might be able to shed some light on her dad's life. Cass was stronger now, and the confidence she had gained knowing that her father had indeed loved her emboldened her. She was no longer afraid of the truth, whatever it might reveal.

Juggling the baby and the business card, she had dialed Ray Stevens, as the card identified him. Torn between relief and disappointment, she left a voice mail stating her name and the person she was inquiring about. Less than an hour later, her phone rang and as she looked at the number in the caller I.D., her heart began to pound. The blood rushing through her ears competed with his voice.

"Is this Cass Parker?"

"Y-yes," her voice faltered. "Mr. Stevens?"

"Call me Ray."

"Ray. I understand you may have known my father? I found your business card in his backpack."

"When did you come into possession of his backpack, Ms. Parker?"

"Last July, two police officers delivered it to my office. I am in Indiana. They said it was the only thing worth saving when they found his body in January."

"Ms. Parker, did they say where they found him?"

"Frozen in his car, outside Luna, Ohio."

Cass could hear a pen scratching paper as the conversation paused.

"I see. Ms. Parker, what was your relationship with your father?"

"I haven't seen him since he left when I was seven years old. I'm not sure why I'm telling you this, but until that backpack was delivered, I didn't care if I ever saw him again. I was dealing with a lot of unresolved anger towards him. What kind of man leaves his wife and kid? But in that pack was a letter he had written, and after reading that, and talking more with my mother, I learned that I didn't have all the facts. Living with my mom had left things pretty one-sided."

"Hm . . . mmm" He said to assure her of his interest. "I can imagine that was very difficult for you growing up."

"Anyway, I was looking in his backpack again, wishing things might've been different. I have a four month old son, Jason Landry. I need to know what kind of man he really was."

"Ms. Parker, what would you say if I told you I had information best delivered in person? Would you be willing to meet with me? In a public place, of course. Your choosing."

After a few phone calls confirming dates and location, Cass was on her way. Pulling into the parking lot of the Waffle Shoppe in Patton Ohio, Cass was grateful to be a few minutes early. She took the baby to the restroom to get him into a fresh diaper and prepared a bottle just in case he woke up in a squall. She tucked the blankets around his little pink face crowned by jet black fuzz, overcome by the serenity she felt gazing at him. A miracle. Her miracle.

Exiting the rest room, the creak of the swinging door announcing her, she saw a tall man in a sport coat rubbing his hands together. Brown hair curled over his collar, identifying him as younger than she'd assumed from their conversations. Taking a chance, she introduced herself.

"Ray? I'm Cass. Sandy, you may have heard."

Cass gave him a long look, certain she knew him from somewhere. Is he staring at me because I'm staring at him, or was he staring first?

He signaled the hostess to lead them to a table, requesting something private. They each ordered coffee.

"I believe this is the second cup of coffee I've bought you." Chuckling at her confused expression, he continued. "Hair in pony tail, big sunglasses. Having a rough day, if I remember correctly."

"No way." Cass said. "That's impossible! That was you? What were you doing in Indiana?"

"Visiting my brother. That's his gas station."

"So, uh, you knew my dad?" Flushing, Cass turned the conversation to safer ground.

"I did know your dad. I always knew him to be a good man, a man who loved Jesus."

Her throat tightened as she listened to him describe a man she did not know. Apparently after leaving them, he had enlisted in the military, failing to find work any place else. He was on the edge of being too old, but since enlistments were down, they were willing to accept him. Lan, as Ray called him, had stayed in the Army as long as they allowed, then was honorably discharged to nothing at all. No home to return to, no job willing to take him, he ended up on the streets for awhile, in and out of shelters in the central Ohio region. Lan was always willing to work, Ray assured her, but jobs for men his age were in short supply.

He'd been able to buy a car with some Social Security money he'd saved up, living in it when he couldn't get a room. Ray had been working with him for a few years, trying to help him find permanent housing.

"You said he was a man who loved Jesus. That is not the way I remember him." She said directly. "What happened?"

"Well, when he was staying at the rescue mission in the city, a different church would come each week to do a service and work in the dining room. He began to listen, and well, all I can say is that the message broke through. I only knew him after that, but from what he says, he is a changed man. The man you describe and the man I know sound like two different men, but that isn't the case."

Something he said triggered an alarm.

"You just said 'the man I know'. Ray, my father is dead. The police found him frozen in his car."

"Cass, I don't know how to tell you this, but that man they found in your dad's car was not your dad."

The room spun as Cass grasped the air in front of her. This cannot be happening.

219

"What did you just say?" she choked.

"The Thanksgiving before last, your dad picked up a man who said he needed a ride to the holiday meal the rescue mission was putting on. That man ended up beating your dad and stealing his car. When I caught up with him, your dad was living in the YMCA, healing from his wounds. Nothing life threatening, but a fractured cheek bone and a broken nose are not things a seventy-five year old man heals from overnight.

"Are you telling me my dad is alive?" Cass whispered hoarsely.

Nodding, Ray said "Would you like to meet him?"

Not trusting her voice, Cass nodded. Good thing she was sitting as she felt her knees melt into her shoes.

Ray stood and nodded towards the vestibule by the front door. Her back to the entrance, Cass slowly rose from the booth and turned.

Landry Alan Parker was not as tall as she remembered. Silver hair combed neatly across the top of his head, obviously a fresh hair cut. Pink skin reminiscent of a baby's, freshly shaved, the faintest silver stubble glistening on the spots he'd missed. He walked slowly, the large brown shoes on his feet almost comical. His dark green polyester coat, the kind with the nappy fur hood, hung open revealing a belt cinched tight around his waist. A blue plaid flannel shirt with the triangle of his undershirt showing.

Her father.

She met his eyes, the deep blue she remembered as a child, brimming with unshed tears.

"Sandy," he said softly. "Just as beautiful as I knew you'd be."

Cass swallowed rapidly, not trusting her voice. She had dreamed of this moment her whole life. In all her fairy tales, she could not have written this better. The scripture that Lauren was always quoting came to her mind, "Now to Him who is able to do more than we can ask or imagine, to Him be the glory."

"Amen," she whispered. "Amen."

"Who's this?" he said huskily, gesturing toward the tiny bundle in the crook of her arm.

"Dad," she tasted the word, strange on her tongue, "Dad, this is my son. Jason Landry Parker."

He looked up in surprise, unable to keep the tears at bay any longer. "You gave him my name?"

Cass just nodded, opening her free arm to engulf her father, the three of them lost in an embrace almost thirty years in the making. He smelled of Aqua Velva as she had remembered. The restaurant, Ray, the years, all seemed to fade away as they held each other.

"I'm so sorry, Sandy, I'm so sorry," her dad cried into her shoulder. "I'm so sorry."

"Dad, no regrets, right? They're too heavy to carry. There will be time to talk later."

After motioning the waitress over, a round of fresh coffee and pie in front of them, Cass began the long conversation of filling her father in on all he had missed. He told her some stories from his military days, stories of when he knew her mother as a teenager.

"Dad, I came across the letters *PYM* written in your Bible. *PYM?*"

"Park your mind. It's learning to park your mind on the things God wants you to, instead of letting it wander around on you. It's how I survived," he said, with a faraway look, his eyes haunted by things unspoken.

The shadows grew long as an idea began to form in Cass's mind. Why not, she thought. Just why not?

"Dad," she said aloud, "What would you think about continuing this conversation at home?"

A grin she hadn't seen since she was a child broke out across his face.

"I would like that very much. Very much." He reached into his coat pocket. "Butterscotch?"

CHAPTER 31

Cass stood on the stage of Brooke Besor, her church, looking at the sea of faces, some of whom she called friends already. *Brooke Besor*, Lauren had explained, was the place David's soldiers rested when they were too exhausted to continue the battle. "We want people to experience this church as a place of rest and rejuvenation, a place to recharge their souls for the battles they face." It had become exactly that for Cass.

Pastor Mike addressed the congregation, thanking everyone for coming to support Cass as she dedicated her son to the Lord. After a short ceremony, highlighted by the squeals of delight from Jase, he invited the friends and family, and anyone else who felt lead to do so, to stand in support of Cass as she raised her son to know the Lord.

Cass's vision swam in tears as she watched Mack and her mother, diamond ring glinting even at a distance, her father and Ray Stevens, and Lauren and her teen-aged sons, Caroline, and Shelby, along with her husband and kids, Jase's cousins as they called themselves, rise immediately in their pews. Slowly, a wave crossed the congregation as more people stood in support of Cass, an outpouring of welcome and love to this family. Cass even spotted Dr. Basara in the crowd.

Pastor Mike invited everyone to bow their heads as he prayed over Cass and her son.

"Father God, we lift up this mother to you, knowing the road she has traveled already. We know that even as we speak, her daughter is worshiping in your presence, waiting for the day this family will stand in the arms of eternity together. For today, though, please strengthen Cass for the tasks that lie ahead. Please bless her with wisdom as she navigates life as a single mother, helping her to make wise decisions that honor you. Please bless her with courage, as I know you have already, for the days that we don't understand.

"For Jason Landry, please instill in him a love for you, Father, to guide him along paths of righteousness. Bless them with friends and mentors to speak wisdom into both of their lives. Give them both a hunger to know You as You lead them in the way everlasting. I ask this blessing in the Name of Your Son, Jesus Christ. And all God's people said, Amen."

EPILOGUE

Jase lead the way to the nursery, accustomed to helping his mother keep the toddlers corralled during the last church service each weekend. The five-year-old knew he had been a twin and occasionally felt like he was missing something, like he'd misplaced a beloved toy. Playing with the kids in the nursery filled an emptiness he didn't have the words or maturity to fully explain.

Cass watched her son proudly. He seemed especially drawn to the dark haired boy playing alone. Mano, his tag said. His first time in the nursery, the boy was putting up a brave front, and her son seemed sensitive to him. Staring at the two dark heads intent on building the biggest block tower possible, she was struck by the similarities. He must have some Polynesian ancestry, Cass mused.

Crosstown Church had been their home for the last three years, since moving closer to the VA hospital for her dad's health care. Cass felt comfortable here; serving in the nursery helped heal the place in her heart Jada had left. Not that Jase wasn't enough . . . he was. She knew she would never fully get over burying a child.

Snapped out of her reverie by a sudden toddler squall, she focused her attention on the kids. The time passed quickly as she directed or redirected as the case required, read stories, served the requisite fish shaped crackers, and made sure every child felt special and welcome.

Voices in the hallway set off a flurry of activity in the nursery; the kids seemed to know instinctively that their parents were on the way. As the adults made their way to the counter, Cass guessed the pretty dark haired woman to be the mother of their newest guest by the similarity in their appearances.

Thick waist length hair, sparkling brown eyes, and perfectly straight teeth flashed in a welcoming smile. Cass would not have been surprised to see her pull a lei out of her purse in greeting.

Something unsettled her about this woman. Probably just the ethnic tie to Cato, a name she didn't allow herself to think about.

Cass flashed her own friendly smile at Mano's mom, extending her hand in greeting. "I'm Cass. I don't believe I've met you or your son before. Welcome to Crosstown."

"Thank you. Melania, but my friends call me Lani for short. This is our second time here, but the first time bringing Mano to the nursery. He seems to have survived," she said with a laugh. "Looks like he made a friend, too."

"That's my son, Jase. He enjoys helping in here with me."

Jase lead Mano to the exit and handed off his new friend. She swept him up with a smile over her shoulder. "Let's go find daddy and make sure he doesn't eat all the donuts before we get there. Say 'see you next week,' Mano."

"See you next week, Mano," giggled the little boy.

Cass glanced down at her son as Lani disappeared around the corner with Mano, surprised to see a wistfulness in his eyes. "What is it, buddy?"

226

"Nothing. It's just, sometimes, I wish . . . nevermind." He flashed a quick smile at his mom. He hugged her around the waist, hiding his face against her.

"I know, bud. I know." Cass knew she wasn't the only one that felt the emptiness Jada left behind. "How about we stop for the biggest sundaes we can find on the way home? Extra cherries even, just for today. And, I have some news that just might put a bigger smile on your face than cherries."

Just then Ray ducked into the nursery. "Ready to go, Mrs. Stevens?" he called, reaching for Cass's hand.

"Dad, mom says we are stopping for sundaes!" Jase yelled excitedly. "Big ones, with extra cherries even!"

In Fellowship Hall, Lani had no trouble spotting her husband. His face broke out in a broad smile as he saw his wife and son heading his direction. "Mel, Mano, what took you so long? I almost ate all the donuts!"

"I think I made a friend. Her name is Cass. I'll have to introduce you next week. Her son seems to have some Island blood in him, and he made a great playmate for Mano."

Cato stopped in his tracks, fear and disbelief each pulling for control of his features. "Couldn't be," he muttered.

"What'd you say, babe?"

"Nothing. Let's go," Cato said with a backwards glance down the nursery hall, as he pulled his family towards the exit.

REFLECTION/DISCUSSION QUESTIONS

1. Cass grew up assuming she was not "Jesus" material. Why do you think she felt this way? What changed her perception?
2. How did the absence of Cass's father in her life affect her relationships with men and God? How have your circumstances defined your relationships with God and other people?
3. Why was Caroline so upset with God? Have you ever felt "let down" by God? How did you deal with the situation?
4. Which character do you think grew the most spiritually, Cass or Caroline? What is the evidence of their growth, in your eyes? Do you think Cass would have been able to forgive her parents without knowing Christ? How about Caroline?
5. Growing up, I belonged to a church that stressed rules over grace and forgiveness. After some issues, I thought God was through with me. Have you ever felt like that? Take some time to journal about your experience or share it with a trusted friend. Where are you now?

A NOTE FROM THE AUTHOR

While this book is not an autobiography, I can relate to many of the experiences of my characters. I grew up in a single-parent family, and was sexually abused by an adult neighbor in my elementary school years. I took all the hurt and shame and buried it deep, never realizing that the feelings I was ignoring were being played out in my choices every day. I never cut, but I relieved the emptiness and anger I carried through living a promiscuous lifestyle, even after I married. I searched for significance the only way I knew how.

When I looked at my life, I saw nothing that Jesus Christ could want, so I continued to live far from Him.

What I learned, though, was that not only was He not mad at me, as I had feared, but that He actually desired a relationship with me. He didn't need me to change or clean up my act before coming to Him, either. He brought about the changes that healed my deepest hurts. In Him, I found freedom.

If you are dealing with painful experiences in your past, you are not alone. You might want to check out these resources:

Healing Hearts is a compassionate outreach to men and women who have been wounded by their past. They offer studies and groups that deal with past sexual abuse and post-abortion counseling. You can find them at <u>www.</u><u>healinghearts.org</u>.

Celebrate Recovery is a Christ-centered program offering help with many addictive and self-destructive behaviors. There are groups for those living out the behaviors as well as those affected by them.

The most impactful thing I learned about Jesus Christ is that He doesn't save just for eternity. He is the hope, encouragement, and sustenance I need for my life every day. All the sin, all the searching . . . I know now that it was an attempt to fill a hole that only He can.

I pray that if you are not in a relationship with Him, you will hear Him calling out to *you*. He knows *your* name.

Debbie Giese

CPSIA information can be obtained at www.ICGtesting.com
Printed in the USA
LVOW12s1133160713

342986LV00002BA/2/P